down
to the
bone

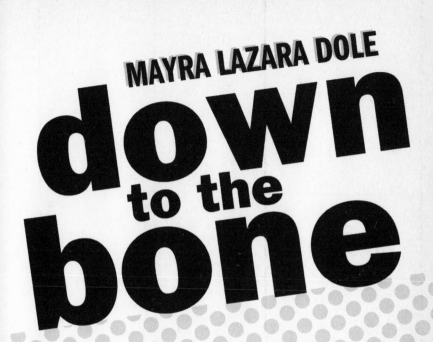

MAYRA LAZARA DOLE

down
to the
bone

HARPER TEEN *An Imprint of HarperCollinsPublishers*

HarperTeen is an imprint of
HarperCollins Publishers.

Library of Congress Cataloging-in-Publication Data
is available.
ISBN 978-0-06-084310-6 (trade bdg.)
ISBN 978-0-06-084311-3 (lib. bdg.)

Typography by Jennifer Heuer
1 2 3 4 5 6 7 8 9 10
❖
First Edition

Every word in this book is **dedicated** to you, my **beautiful Damarys**, and to **Mami**, *la mejor madre del mundo*. You'll both live within me till forever.

M.L.D.

Acknowledgments

Damarys, this novel exists because you quit your career in order to help keep me alive after I was chemically injured. Your unrelenting support, selfless dedication, love, and encouragement mean so much to me. Words could never express my enormous debt of gratitude and appreciation for your loving devotion and for all you've done and sacrificed for me.

Janell Walden Agyeman, my agent, your support, time, attention, listening skills, and positive outlook make you an outstanding agent in my eyes. Rosemary Brosnan, my gifted and talented editor, I can't thank you enough for taking on my novel, for believing in my cause, and for being a person and editor of integrity. I feel privileged to have worked with you and have deep respect for you. And Mami, if it weren't for you and your heartfelt care, love, and endless support, I wouldn't be alive today. I love you with all my heart and soul!

I'd also like to thank my loving friends for always being supportive and caring: Coky and Paul Michel, Beba, Teresa Rodriguez, and C. J. Buffalo. A special thanks to Sil and to Robert Cava.

Finally, I'd like to thank the following people who read my manuscript and helped in whatever small or large way they could: DeeDee, Maude, Michael, Ian, TZ, Xena, Ita, Maria Gomez, and every single person at HarperCollins who worked on my book.

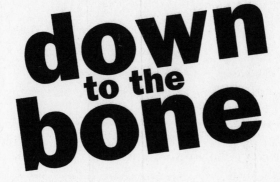

The Kiss

This morning the sun rose like a loaf of sweet banana bread. That's because today is the last day of school and we're free before lunch! And if *that's* not the best news ever, check *this* out: it's my two-year anniversary with Marlena, the love of my life. Her summer vacation started yesterday. She's expecting me at her place so we can celebrate. I can't *wait* to get out of this boring last class to visit her!

Sister Asunción—better known as Fart Face—is at the board writing the titles of the texts we'll need next year. What kind of a wacked-out thing is *that*? I'm secretly reading the love letter Marlena gave me yesterday. I've got it hidden inside my math book.

> Scrunchy,
>   Happy anniversary! I never thought I could love someone soooooo much. Remember our first kiss?

I close my eyes.

Wild, galloping rain and booming thunder shake my apartment. Pedri, my little bro, is spread out on the orange living-room sofa watching MTV. Mami and her boyfriend, Osvaldo, sit in the garlic-smelling dining room, yacking and drinking after-dinner cafecitos. Marlena and I are chillin' on my bed, listening to hip-hop.

She tells me, "My dad's crazy to think rap is evil."

"Yeah. I wish he wasn't so strict

and let you come to parties with me." I shake my head. "He's so messed up."

She smoothes my hair away from my face and kisses my forehead. "That's why I love coming here." Her black eyes sparkle. "Dancing with you is what kissing must be like: the best feeling in the world." With a flick of the finger, she changes the music to a slow, romantic bolero and just lies there looking into my eyes.

I bolt from the bed, rush to the music shelf, grab a Cuban CD, and put it on. Heart-thumping beats vibrate the walls.

I hoist my button-down hip-hugger jeans and mess up my long, straight black hair so it's crazy-wild. "Come on!"

Marlena jolts out of bed and lands in front of me. She tries to mimic my wild, freestyle footwork and bouncy rhythm, but her feet get all tangled up. I rotate my hips before stepping into a twirling cha-cha-cha. "Super-slick or what?"

"You're the best!" She jams up the music. "I'm going to break-dance."

"You? To this *music?*" I let out a piercing laugh. "Right! And I'm growing a pin-striped eyeball on the tip of my nose."

"You'll see!" She stands on her head and stares up at me from the floor.

"A dry head spin? No *way!* You'll break your neck! Start with the six steps."

She doesn't listen and lands smack on her chunky butt.

We laugh our heads off.

The CD ends, and for a second there's a sharp silence. We stand face-to-face. A whooshing wind dives in through the bedroom windows, *making her long, jet-black curls wave around in the breeze. We look deeply into each other's eyes. Her black eyes seem liquid under the dim light of my purple lava lamp. A beautiful sweetness pours over me, reminding me that she's becoming one of my closest friends.*

The walls around me fade. I feel as if I'm swimming inside her soul. Something different is happening inside me. She leans into me. Her velvety lips touch mine, and I get goose bumps all over. I feel as if silvery threads of rain are covering my entire body. I'm turning into the sea, becoming one with her, melting.

We kiss for a long, long time.

I stroke Marlena's face with my hands and outline her lips with my fingers. . . .

"Didn't you hear my question?" I'm snapped cold out of my thoughts when a looming shadow stands in my way. I look up. *¡Ay, ay, ay!* Gray-haired, wrinkly Fart Face tears Marlena's letter out of my hands. My heart thumps in my chest something furious.

She faces the class. "Would you like to hear what's in this highly important letter?"

She can't read the letter out loud. She *can't*!

"Yeah!" everyone except my best friend, Soli, blasts.

"Please give it back." I try to grab the letter forcefully out of her hands, but instantly she pulls it away.

Fart Face puts on a disgustingly fake smile and walks slowly to her desk. "So this letter is *that* good, huh?" She sits poised on the chair, lowers her reading glasses, and reads:

> "You're the greatest kisser in the
> world, Scrunchy. I can't wait till
> tonight, when your family leaves for
> your grandmother's, so we can be
> alone and make love."

The guys whistle and shout, "Way to go!

Scrunchy is finally hooking up!"

Fart Face walks toward me with almost silent steps. She stops a few feet away from my desk. "Wait until your mother finds out. She'll just *love* it." She turns to the class.

"Should I continue reading, or is this too boring?"

"Read on!" Everybody except Soli goes nuts. She sits wagging her head.

"No! Please, stop," I beg with my heart in my mouth.

"Quiet!" Fart Face stomps her foot and shuts me up.

My whole body quivers. I want to run for my life, but my feet are glued to the floor.

She clears her raspy voice and continues . . .

> "I feel I've known you all my life, and I
> know we'll be together till eternity.
> You mean everything to me, Scrunchy."

"Scrunch-Munch is a beast!" Rodrigo cheers.

"Scrunch-Munch! Scrunch-Munch!" the guys yell.

Soli is widening her eyes as if telling me, "Grab the letter and run!" But I can't move.

"Every day I love you more. I'm glad
you love me too. I can feel it deep,
deep in my heart."

Rigoberto teases, "Who's your secret lovey-dove, huh, Scrunchy?"

My chest hurts as if a Mack truck is parked on it. I think about a white horse picking me up and galloping me full speed out of here. Mami's going to kill me. They're going to expel me from school. I've got to do *some*thing before everyone finds out!

"What we have is special. . . ."

I'm trapped by Fart Face's rasping voice, hurting my ears, killing me slowly. She's really enjoying this. I know that the line that's coming is going to be the end of me.

I cover my face with my hands.

"I know we are girls, but a guy could

never make love to me the way you do. I never thought being with a girl could bring so much pleasure. I love you with all my heart and soul. I'll love you till forever, my beautiful Laura Sofía. . . ."

After a roaring "What?" the room becomes hushed.

I feel darts shooting at me from my friend Cecilia's eyes as she shouts, "You're a *tortillera*?"

My good friend Yasi snaps, "Revolting!"

Aracelis's stare pierces right through me. "I can't be*lieve* we've been your friends all these years and you *never* told us."

Bookworm Margarita speaks up. "Give her a break. Don't be so dense. It's no big deal."

"Wait till she wants to hook up with *you*!" Olivia remarks. She sticks her index finger in her mouth as if she were about to puke.

I gulp down my pain and put on a stern "I don't care" face. I won't give them the satisfaction of seeing me hurt.

Soli rushes over and puts an arm around my

shoulder. "Hey, jerks. We're in the twenty-first century. So *what* if she's homo. Don't you *morons* watch MTV?" She gives attitude just by being her curvy self, with those big watermelon boobs, flat stomach, tiny waist, and double-basketball bootie.

Gustavo lets out a gutsy laugh. "I got no problem hooking up with lesbos. Let's have a threesome!"

"Yeah!" The guys get all riled up, laughing hysterically, clapping and stomping their feet. "Let's do it! *Three*some! *Three*some!"

"Shush!" Fart Face reprimands. She juts her long, pointy chin at Soli. "Go back to your seat, Soledad."

Soli squeezes me harder to her.

Fart Face untangles Soli's arm from around me and raises her voice. "Laura, follow me."

As I head out the door, Cecilia spits in my face. "*¡Tortillera!*"

Mother Superior-Sicko

Fart Face walks her Godzilla self into Mother Superior's office, dragging me behind her. What am I going to do? I *have* to get out of here!

Mother Superior-Sicko—a cockroach of a nun, with bloodshot, steely eyes; paper-thin lips; and tangled eyebrows—stands with feet planted close together as she reads the letter. I want to tear it out of her hands, but she'll kill me.

She calls Mami at the factory and says in Spanish, "Mrs. Amores, we have a problem with your daughter. She's in the office due to an immoral issue. We need you here immediately."

That call is my death. My legs feel as if they're made of clay; I can hardly stand.

To Mami, being a homo is the worst thing in the world. She'd rather I chop off someone's head and get life imprisonment, or fry in the chair, than be a daughter who's in love with another girl.

I can't stop my hands from trembling. I've got to pee so bad. Sweat drips down my back from my neck as I wait for Mami to come through the door. No one is talking to me. But they're talking about me:

"This is pre*post*erous. One bad apple will spoil our impeccable reputation. We can't allow indecency in our moral school."

I raise my hand. In a quavering voice, with trembling lips, I say. "May I please use the restroom?" I'll make a mad dash out of this messed-up school and run for my life after I pee.

Mother Superior-Sicko grits her teeth. She scratches her lightbulb-shaped nose.

"The *rest*room? You should have *thought* about the *con*sequences of this letter, young lady." Her ears and neck flush a dark pink. A thick blue vein on her forehead pops out. Her eyes drill holes into mine. "Hold it until we resolve this matter."

I try to sit down, but they won't let me. My legs are weak. My insides are shaking something awful.

Before you know it, Mami rushes in through the door, and Fart Face is reading the letter to her.

"*I'll love you till beyond eternity . . .*"
"*You know who . . .*"

Mami explains in a nervous tone, "Why, this can't be. She likes boys. Laura takes ballet. She wears dresses."

Mother Superior-Sicko glares at me. She points a fat finger toward the middle of my forehead. "You must keep watch over Laura so she doesn't meet up with that girl again. They must stop this deviant behavior."

I take a deep breath and hold it. Maybe I'll collapse and die in front of Fart Face. I mean, what would happen then? Would she feel guilty? Would everyone say, "Good riddance. A girl who loves another girl is a worthless piece of crap anyway"?

I exhale when Fart Face comes over to me, shoving the letter in my face. "Laura, who's the girl you kissed and had sex with?"

I want to blurt, "It's your favorite niece, Alicita, the perfect genius you're always yacking about." But instead I zip my lips tightly.

Mami isn't saying a word. This might be the first time in her life she's quiet about anything.

Mother Superior-Sicko gives me an ultimatum: "Tell us who the other culprit is or you'll be expelled." I'm still mute. She continues with hatred in her eyes. "We hear it's trendy to be homosexual, but not in our academy. I won't have sinful girls in this school; that's not the way God intended it."

The ticking sound of the grandfather clock blasts out like a bunch of loud shots, over and over again, driving me crazy.

"She's not sinful and neither am I!" I scream. My tears stream down like an open faucet. No one's going to talk shit about *my* Marlena. I don't give a royal banana if they keep me prisoner here for a million years. I'll *never* talk!

Mami says, "I'm deeply sorry. I raised her to be polite. She's never given me trouble. Laura's been a great girl and a good student. I don't know what's gotten into her."

"I'm not shocked," Fart Face affirms. "Erratic behavior is expected when one is leading a secret, immoral lifestyle. Teens like her, and her perverse girlfriend, need to be stopped before they become more mentally unstable and too troubled to be cured."

Mother Superior-Sicko's jaw is tight as her stare digs holes into my pupils. "Well, Laura Amores, I see that you will not cooperate. You are lucky that today is the last day of school and you've graduated from eleventh grade. But you're not welcome back next year." She blinks her crusty bug eyes. "Get your books and go home."

Mami stays behind, yapping with the Psycho Nuns from Hell. I don't want to see her face when I get back. Maybe I can run into the street and get hit by a car. No. No. Pedri will suffer if I die.

First I dash into the bathroom to pee. Then I walk into the class. Girls stare at me with question marks in their eyes. Guys make fun of me. "Yo, here's Muff Diver!" They laugh like hell and sing out, "Laura eeats octa-pussy! Laura looves octa-pussy!"

"Shut up, jerks!" Soli chews them out.

The room fills with the buzzing sound of gossip. I don't understand. Some of these kids have been my friends all my life.

Soli hugs me and kisses my cheek. "Things'll be okay. I'll call you tonight." Lucky for Soli, everyone knows she's boy crazy, otherwise they'd think *she* was the "Evil Culprit." I don't want her to let go. I want her to slap me awake and tell me this isn't real.

I kiss her cheek. "Later." The lump in my throat is killing me.

I grab my book bag and see smiles on the faces of Margarita, Julian, Sasha, and Hernando. "*Hasta luego*, Laura."

"Bye." I wave back to them, then to everyone else, but most look away.

"Disgusting!" Cecilia yells after me. Another voice calls, "Lying dyke!"

I hear Soli shouting, "Leave her alone, asswipes!"

I close the door behind me, knowing what my life will be like from now on: pure hell on wheels.

We're in Mami's prehistoric *cacharro*. The fumes are making me nauseous. She puts her foot to the pedal, grips the wheel, and prays, "*Ay, Jesucristo, give me strength*." She tears the tiny, plastic San Lázaro statue from the dashboard, holds it against her heart, and makes a *promesa*: "If you save my child from homosexuality, I'll never cut my hair for as long as I live."

Cuban mothers always make weird promises like that. I mean, what saint would give three-and-a-half bananas if Mami let her hair grow down to her heels?

On our way home I try to reason with her: "Let me explain."

She yanks my hair. "Explain? You're a dis*grace* to our family name. If your father were alive, he'd

17

die right now. Tell me who that *degenerada* girl is!"

I stare out the window, mute. No way will I tell. That'll start World War III.

The rest of the ride is in silence.

We get home and walk into Mami's dark, hair-spray-scented bedroom. She pulls up the shades, and the light blinds me. I cover my eyes with my forearm.

"So *that's* what you've been doing for two years when we've left for Abuela's, eh?" Mami shakes her head in disgust. *"¡Dios mío!"* Tears stream down her face. "I've never been so humiliated and embarrassed in all my life."

I stand by the bed and look down at my two-tone school shoes. I can't believe she didn't defend me when they were calling me an evil sicko. But no way will I fight back. She'll slap the brain juice right out of my head.

She picks up her loose hair, twists it into a large bun at the back of her head, and sticks bobby pins deep into it. "Which of your school friends is it—Soli, Yasi, Aracelis, or Cecilia?"

I keep quiet. Marlena goes to La Caridad del

Cobre High School, and her dad never once allowed her to sleep over. What a damned lucky break that Mami and the Nuns from Hell believe it's someone from my school. Mami might never figure out who the "Evil Culprit" is.

There's a huge silence. Abruptly, we hear Pedri's school bus leaving him in front of the house. Mami walks into the living room. I hear Pedri open the door and run to Mami for a hug. "Go to your room and stay until I'm done with your sister."

He obeys.

She barges into the bedroom again and waves her hands in the air. "So, you're still not talking, eh? That despicable girl gets to finish high school at Virgen María High, and *you* get thrown out?"

Her high heels *clickety clack* loudly in my ears as she paces the room, back and forth, back and forth. My head feels as if it's going to crack open.

"Until you tell me who you've been having indecent, immoral sex with in *my* house, you won't be allowed to leave the house, bring friends over, or talk on the phone." Her voice rises in a frightening tone. "I just got married to Osvaldo. Tomorrow we begin our honeymoon, the first vacation I've had in six years; and you do this to me *now*? He better *never* find out or he'll divorce me. A woman needs a man, and I've started my life again. Don't you *dare* ruin my chances of staying with him!"

She snatches my cell phone from my book bag and storms off to the kitchen. Pedri runs to me from his room. "What happened, Laury? Why is Mami so mad?"

I sit him on my lap and hold him tightly against me. I need to feel his love around me.

"Little Punk, they threw me out of school." I hug him closer, tighter, as I gulp hard and try not to cry.

He searches my eyes while holding on to the back of my neck with both hands. "Were you bad?"

I kiss the tip of his little marble-shaped nose, press my forehead against his, and look into his eyes, which are the color of green bubble gum. "Nope. They threw me out cuz I won't tattle on a friend. Don't worry about it, okay?" I brush his golden curls away from his forehead with my fingers and squeeze my cheek to his. He's all mushy and marshmallowy.

Pedri smiles, showing his tiny teeth and one missing front tooth. "Okay."

Mami calls him, and he rushes off.

I go to my room, shut the door behind me, and throw myself on the bed. I hear Mami in the kitchen, slamming cabinet doors and banging pots and pans. It's safe to make a quick call to Marlena.

I grab the cordless phone from my night table and dial Marlena's number.

She answers. *"¿Oigo?"*

I whisper everything that happened in detail, without stopping for a single breath.

"Oh, my God! I should never have written you that letter. I'm so sorry."

"It's not your fault. *I* was the nitwit who was reading it in class. I should have known better." I whisper words that pour out of me. "Everybody hates me now just because I'm in love with you.

Mami is treating me like a criminal. My friends are never going to talk to me again. How could this crazy crap be happening?"

"Oh, Scrunchy." She sighs loudly. "What are we going to do?"

"Don't worry. No one found out about you, and no one *ever* will." I don't want her to get nervous.

"I'm glad I didn't sign the letter. That's the smartest thing I've ever done. Can you imagine?" Her voice trembles. "I'm relieved no one knows it's me. This way we can still see each other and work it through. You'll see."

I pull off my blouse, ball it up, and throw it against a wall. It's suffocating me.

Everybody's hatred is still stuck to it.

"Everything's going really wrong. I wish things were back to normal."

"You're out of that school already. Just transfer to a different one where people don't know you."

"But I *love* my friends, and I want them to love me again. I want to show them I'm not a freak like they think." I massage my head. It's throbbing intensely. "Loving you is the most beautiful thing *ever*; it isn't the ugliest, most disgusting thing like they want me to believe. They're wacked."

An abrupt, loud scream comes through the receiver. "Laura! Who's the degenerate you love so much on the other end of this line, eh? Speak, *degenerada*. Speak!"

Falling Sky

Mami slams down the phone and storms into my room. "How *dare* you talk to that girl behind my back after everything you've just put me through?"

I grab my favorite red tank top—the one I wear to sleep—from under my pillow and slide it on. I sit on my bed with my head lowered. I've heard that you never look into a barking, rabid dog's eyes or it'll get more vicious and might attack and kill you.

Mami arches her eyebrows and breathes fast and heavy. "My friends' daughters are all *normal*. It's humiliating to be the *only* person I know whose daughter was thrown out of Catholic school"—she clears her throat—"because she's *ab*normal." She slaps my thigh with her hand. "Tell me once and for all, Laura Sofía Lorena, who were you just talking to?"

"Let's forget about it, Mami, please." I can't lift my head to look at her. I wish I hadn't called Marlena till Mami was in bed with Osvaldo, asleep. What an idiot I am. I'm empty-headed, brainless, stupid!

She points in the direction of the front door. "If you won't tell me, then leave!"

"Mami, no. Please," I beg. All I need is to be thrown out of my own house.

"Go! Get out of here until you decide to tell me who the culprit is. Go!"

Like a crazed animal, she tears my clothes and shoes from my closet and throws them on my bed. My laptop gets stashed in my closet. She opens all the drawers and piles my underwear, CDs, some old records, and shoulder bag on top of my art stuff.

"I've begged you enough to tell me who the girl is. I don't want you living in this household till you come clean and you've changed!"

"*¡Mami, por favor, por favor!*" I run around after her. She stuffs all my things in my shoulder bag and in a huge garbage bag. She rushes into the living room, opens the front door, and throws everything out.

"Go," she says with tears in her eyes. "See if your secret lover's parents will take you in." Her veins swell and pop out on her neck. "Have *them* pay all your bills, love you, and care for you as I have."

Pedri, hearing all the commotion through the open windows, runs to me from the swings in the backyard. "Laury, what happened?"

Mami screeches out an explanation about my being bad. "She knows what she must do in order to come back." She wipes her tears with the back of her arm.

"Don't throw Laury away, Mami, please." Pedri holds on to me. "Don't go, Laury," he bawls.

"Mami, I promise." I fall on my knees, tears gushing from my eyes. "I'll never talk to any of my friends again."

She doesn't listen. "I'll tell Osvaldo I let you stay at a friend's house for the summer. Don't forget to take your dog." She goes to the laundry room, where Chispita has her bed, and wakes her up. She practically throws her to me.

Pedri hugs me hard and runs to his room, sobbing.

Mami pushes me out the front door. I stumble and almost fall, but I don't. "I'm sorry, Laura, but I can't continue loving you if you stay gay." She calms down a little. "I love you with all my being. I'm doing this for your own good. When you've changed and you're honest with me about who the girl is, come back."

She slams the door in my face.

A bunch of sparrows fly overhead. There's a weird brown ring around the clouds. I think the sky is going to fall. I have an odd sensation in my chest, as if I have a hole in there the size of Cuba.

Tangled and Breathing

"Get in! Fast!" Marlena grabs my arm and pulls me inside. "My family is in Fort Lauderdale. They won't be back for two hours." She kisses my lips. "I love you so much, Scrunchy." She hurriedly takes Chispita out into the fenced backyard with a bowl of water.

We rush into her strawberry-scented office-turned-bedroom. For six months she's been living in Miami Beach with her *tío* Paco, *tía* Hilda, and three cousins. Luckily, she talked her father into letting her stay with her uncle and aunt till she finished high school, while the rest of the family moved back to Puerto Rico.

She gently kisses my entire face. "She doesn't know it was me, right? You didn't tell her, did you?"

I fling myself onto her bouncy bed and softly pull her to me. "Of course not." I lie on top of her and give her sweet kisses on her neck. "I'd never do that to you. I love you."

She tosses her hair away from her face and lowers her deep-set eyes. "You're my life." She plants a moist kiss on my lips. "Tell me *every-thing*."

"She kicked me out. I stashed my stuff behind the front yard bush and got here by bus." I tell her the whole story, in full, vivid detail. "I can't go back home unless I give her the name of the 'Evil Culprit.'"

"Oh, God!" Her eyes pierce mine. "You'll never, *ever* say it's me. Right? She'll tell my uncle. He'll call my dad in Puerto Rico. My whole family will find out." She's talking a mile a minute. "They'll force me to move back. It'll be *hell* for us. I won't ever be allowed to see you again."

"Chill out, Pooki. They'd have to cut my head

off before I'd tell on you."

She rolls me over and lightly sits on my thighs. I love that she's meaty and curvaceous. Her ample hips feel good on me. "I wish you could stay here, but everyone will wonder what's going on."

"I know." I can barely muster the energy to speak.

She leans into me and kisses my earlobe. I love her warm, sweet, familiar breath.

"What will you do? Where will you go? You'll still work part-time with *tío* Paco, right? I *have* to see you every day."

Before I can answer, she rushes to her dainty white desk, takes out a wad of bills from one of the cabinets, and hands them to me. "Three hundred and twelve dollars."

I give them back. "No. I have some money." I don't want to take the money she's been saving to buy a car.

She insists that I take it all and stuffs the bills into my skirt pocket. "Return it if you don't use it."

"Maybe I'll go to Little Havana Hotel."

"You can't afford a hotel. Your money will run

out right away." She kisses my forehead. "I hate your mom for doing this to you. I've never seen you so down. Go to Soli's. She'll take you in. Just remember, you're in my heart. No one will ever tear us apart."

Marlena's the second oldest of five kids and the one responsible for having taken care of her baby brothers and sisters. Her maturity is part of why I love her so much. She means what she says and says what she means, and she'd rather have her eyes poked with needles than lie. I know I can trust her, and I love that feeling.

I wrap my arms around her, and we roll around in bed. She smells delicious, like watermelon candy.

"I can't stay at Soli's. She lives in that tiny duplex. Her bedroom is the size of an ant."

"You know Soli will give you a kidney if you need it."

The thought that Soli and me have been best friends since first grade lifts my spirits a little. But still, I can't be a burden to her and her mom.

Marlena runs her fingers through my hair.

"Your beautiful green eyes look so sad." She kisses my eyelids. "Now that it's summer, come over every day, and on weekends after work, as if nothing's happened. I'll have my uncle drop me off at Soli's on the days you can't visit." I can tell she's worried sick but is trying to make me feel better. She holds my hands in hers. "Just make sure Soli never mentions to anyone that I wrote that letter."

Soli's the only person who knows that Marlena and I are, you know . . . in love. She caught us kissing one day in Marlena's room. We thought Soli was in the bathroom, but she barged in on us unexpectedly and said, "Sweeeet! I knew it all the time!" Marlena freaked, but we all got to talking and Soli promised she'd never tell a single soul. And she hasn't.

I kiss the freckle on Marlena's earlobe and whisper to her, "Is this my freckle?"

She half closes her eyes. "Yours and only yours." Her voice is soft and melodious.

I kiss her forehead, the tip of her nose, down to her mushy lips. We slowly undress each other.

I kiss every cell of her body, from her toes, up to her neck, until I find her mouth.

Time clicks by. We're wrapped around each other under the covers, enveloped in a cocoon of love.

She slips off the delicate silver ring her grandmother gave her before she died and slides it on my ring finger. "Abuelita will help keep you safe." The tiny green emerald set in the center looks like a loving eye watching over me. I feel protected.

A car parks noisily in the driveway. Her older brother, Arturo—the Inquisitor—is visiting from Puerto Rico for the summer.

"Shit!" We bolt out of bed and get dressed fast. I don't feel like talking to him. He asks *way* too many personal questions.

I plop the wad of bills on Marlena's desk when she's not looking and rush to the backyard for Chispita. Marlena follows.

I open the back fence. Chispita leaps all over me as if she hasn't seen me in a million years. "I'll call you from a pay phone."

"Go to Soli's, please. Call me from her place as soon as you get there. I love you," she murmurs. "You're everything to me. I don't want anything to ever happen to you."

I don't tell her I'm not going to Soli's. "I love you more." I hug her tightly and breathe in her delicious scent. I need to take it with me for strength.

Keepin' It Down Low

There's a light aqua sky. The beach is filled with people blasting their boom boxes—people whose lives haven't just been ruined, people who seem normal and happy.

I stand on the pier, looking down, watching my little gum ball chase sand crabs. She runs after them and barks. When she gets close, they disappear into their burrows.

I wish my life were so easy.

I grab Pedri's picture from my shoulder bag. His shiny, smooth face and sweet harmonica smile give me hope. "Laury," he wrote on the back, "you are a big, littol, eskinny, fat, tall, short cooko monthster. I love U berry much! Pedrito."

I walk down to the sand to get Chispita. I throw down my towel and sit under two coconut palms leaning against each other like lovers. The sun sparkles through the fan-shaped greenery. The water laps gently along the shore.

I breathe in the salty smell that reminds me of Mami's cooking. She fries fish every Friday night. I'll probably never eat Mami's home cooking again.

My head is buzzing. I don't know where I'm headed. I hope Marlena's uncle never finds out about "the Incident." I'll lose the full-time summer job he promised me. I really need a job now more than ever.

A girl who looks exactly like a cute surfer boy walks from the water to an empty towel close by. She's wearing a vivid green T-shirt and long bathing trunks. Her straight, bleached blonde hair is buzzed all over, and streaks of dyed purple bangs hang over her eyes. The sleek, dark sunglasses sitting on top of her head make her look hip.

I hope she's not coming toward me. I wouldn't know what to say to a gay girl.

As she nears, Chispita dashes to her. The girl vigorously pets Chispi's fuzzy-wuzzy head. "Hey, cutie," she says in a strong Cuban accent. Chispi is all over her, slobbering her chiseled, dimpled chin and nipping at her tiny earlobes.

"Chispi!" I call. She flies to me and I grab her. "Sorry." I look away into the horizon. I don't want to look into the girl's eyes. She might think I'm into her.

"No problem. I love puppies." She dries her face, wrings the bottom of her T-shirt, and slips on her white sneakers. She brings her purple towel closer to me and plops on it.

"I'm Tazer."

"Tazer?" I've never heard a Cuban with such a name.

"I was born Tazmina, but I hate that name. Everybody calls me Taze or Tazer."

"Hi. I'm Laura." I try hard to crack a smile.

Tazer slides her glasses down to her nose, and her hazel eyes look up over them. I clutch my hair with both hands and stare away from her, into nothingness.

"You okay?" she asks.

"I'm fantastic, feeling fly." I can be a sarcastic pain sometimes.

"What happened?" She catches on.

"Just had a beautiful fight with my mom." I feel my chin trembling. I clutch Chispita in my arms and squeeze her tightly against me.

"That's terrible. Why?"

"Because she's a case." I kiss Chispi's head and stare at the frothy ocean waves. "She's been a case since the day we moved here from Cuba, when I was six."

I don't know why I'm telling a perfect stranger my whole life story, but words just pour out and I can't stop them.

"In first grade I found a book called *Henry and Beezus*. Mami snatched it from me, tore it into pieces, and threw it in the trash. She said, 'Girls who read will become smarter than boys and turn into spinsters who don't have children. They live lonely and miserable lives.'"

Now I know what Mami was talking about. She was saying that no daughter of hers would be a homo.

Tazer totally gets it. *"¡Qué loca!"*

"Yeah. She still wants to tear up my life and throw it away in the garbage."

A bunch of wild green parrots startle us as they circle the palm trees above us. I stand to catch a clearer view. "How beautiful. We had four in Cuba." I want to change the subject from me to anything at all.

Chispita growls and barks up at them. Tazer lifts her, belly up, and pets her chubby tummy. "We've got some wild parrots in our backyard."

It would be rude if I didn't at least ask her *some*thing about herself. She'll just think I'm one of those narcissistic, egocentric, *plástica* Cubanita chicks who don't give a royal rooster's butt about anything but themselves.

I lift my dorky, navy blue school skirt and stretch down my tank top. Too bad Mami didn't give me time to change my skirt. "Where do you live?"

She sets Chispita down on my towel. "I live with my dad, in Gables by the Sea."

Gables by the Sea is one of the richest white places in Miami. "My uncle, who's been here thirty years, got my dad into real estate; and they both struck it rich. I loved living with my family in Cuba, but I hated not being able to speak my mind or travel. I lived in an apartment building with my grandparents, uncles, aunts, and cousins. There were nineteen of us. Now I have everything, but I don't have them."

"Damn. You must miss them like crazy." She nods. I tell her I live in Little Havana. "But soon we're moving to a ritzy neighborhood in Coconut Grove. My mom just got married. She wants to move up in the world." I tell her this so she gets it that I can relate. "I'll miss my old *barrio*, too."

Suddenly I miss Pedri, my home, my *barrio* friends, my school friends, and everyone who now hates me. My chest fills with pain.

Gusts of wind make the coconut palms sway. Sweet smells of fried plantains fill the beach. A vendor walks over to us selling *pastelitos*, *platanitos maduros,* and sodas.

Tazer buys two *pastelitos de guayaba* and two freezing cold Maltas. I thank her and we sit in the shade of the tree, sipping the soda that reminds me of Pedri. When he was a baby, I'd pour condensed milk into a glass bottle, add the Malta, shake it, and feed it to him; it's still his fave.

I take a bite of *pastelito.* "So, what do you do for fun?"

"Surfing, skateboarding, chillin' with other genderqueer friends at the car races, writing plays, and clubbing every weekend with my fake ID." She swallows, wipes *pastelito* flakes off her skinny chicken lips with her hand, and throws me a gleaming smile. "What about you?"

I want to ask what "genderqueer" means, but instead I say, "I love collecting old music and watching foreign movies, especially Cuban and Italian. I'm really into drawing, poetry, painting murals, riding bikes, and stuff like that. I've got a fantastic part-time job doing landscapes, on weekends. Soon Paco, the boss, will be hiring me full-time."

She finishes her *pastelito* and gulps down some Malta. "That's great. I've never seen a foreign movie. Hey"—she licks her lips—"sometime soon my dad will need a landscape estimate. Can I have Paco's phone number?"

"Sure." I give Chispita the last bite of my *pastelito*; she eats it in one gulp and licks my fingers clean. I go into my bag, pull out a piece of paper, write Paco's phone number, and hand the paper to her. "Have your dad call Paco. He's sort of like family. I'm sure he'll give him a great price." It would be fantastic if I could say, "Paco's my uncle-in-law!" But I keep my trap shut.

She stuffs the number in her bathing shorts pocket. "Thanks." She swings her head sideways, trying to get her long bangs out of her eyes. "I need a serious haircut."

I ask for the piece of paper back and write Soli's work number on it. "My friend Soli is the wildest haircutter in town." And it's true. Soli's a beast when it comes to 'dos. She's so popular, she's got lines of people waiting for her at the shop every Friday after school, Saturday mornings, and all summer long. I lift the ends of my long hair. "Don't go by me. I just let her trim the tips."

She stuffs the paper inside her pocket. "Your hair is gorgeous." I look away. Her statement makes me blush. I've never had a compliment from a true-blue gay girl. She notices and changes the topic. "You sure know lots of peeps. I'll give her a call."

It's true. I know hundreds of people *and* their grandmothers! But as of today, I'm not sure who'll want to know *me*.

She points to a fancy hotel with a large, flashing pink neon sign. "That's a gay club. They throw wild parties there, out by the pool, with live merengue and salsa bands. Want to come with me this Saturday night? We'll celebrate the beginning of summer vacation. It'll be a blast."

I feel like she's opening a gate for me, but no way in hell will I go through it.

I shouldn't have come to a gay beach. That was wacko of me. Here I am, terrified of people thinking I'm a *tortillera*. I was thrown out of school *and* my house for loving a girl, and what do I do? I come to a gay beach for the first time in my life. I'm just the most brilliant kid on the block. I'm your typical genie-ass!

"I can't, really. I have a boyfriend, and he hates me going out without him." I lie. What else can I do? Hang out with a butch dyke who looks like a hot guy and have more people hate me? No way, José!

"No problem," she says with an easygoing smile.

I stare out past a gay-girl couple holding hands. I wish that they could be Marlena and me. I look to the two guys taking off their bike gear and helmets, undressing down to their bathing suit trunks. Everyone looks nice and normal, unlike what Mami and most people think.

Tazer squints. "I thought you were queer, coming to this gay beach and all."

"Nope. I've never been here. I came by mistake."

Suddenly I realize that I came looking for a place to belong, where I'm not seen as a freak of nature. I wish I could tell her I wanted to come and see girls openly together, to see why people hate them so much. I'm more confused now than ever, though. I don't understand how everyone on this beach could be so calm and look so joyful. Don't they have families and friends who think they're degenerates? Why aren't they terrified of being seen in public? They're probably tourists. No way a Cuban kid would be "out" in Miami. No way!

"Do your parents know?" I'm curious.

"My mom died giving birth to me."

I lower my eyes. "I'm so sorry."

"It's all right. It happened seventeen years ago."

"How about your dad?"

"Pipo's never home. He doesn't know a thing about me and never asks. He doesn't even know I'm genderqueer."

I can't take not knowing anymore. "What's that?"

She gives out a sweet, boyish laugh. "Ever since I can remember, I always thought myself a real boy, not a girl or a tomboy. I relate to being called "queer," but I don't identify with being lesbian, a dyke, or butch; that would mean I considered myself a girl who likes girls. I see myself a boi—*b-o-i*—who's into girls."

"That's cool." I've seen transgender documentaries. "Are you transitioning?"

"No. I'm scared of operations and hormone shots. I wear an undershirt binder or Ace bandages to press down my chest. Do I look like a butch dyke, an effeminate boy, or a real guy?"

"A typical guy, but I can sorta tell you're a girl. I guess you look like a *b-o-i*."

Her smile widens and gleams something amazing.

The beach fills up with gay Latino kids bringing in blasting music. The guys show off their muscles to other guys while playing football. Cuban girls take off their tight, expensive jeans and high heels. They have on globs of makeup and shiny gold jewelry. You'd think they were going out to a dance club or something. I'm sure none of these kids' parents know they're here, or that they're gay.

Tazer looks at her watch. "Hey, my friend Antonio's been waiting for me. He's having a barbecue at his apartment. We get together *y descargamos* on congas and eat *puerco asado* till midnight. Just like we did in Cuba." She stands and scrubs the sand off her long legs full of light blond peach fuzz. "Want to come along? I know you have a boyfriend and you're straight, but we can be friends, right?"

"Of course." I lie. No way will I be caught dead in the streets with a girl who looks like a boy. "But I can't go now. Maybe some other time." I don't want to tell her I need a place to live. All I need is a boi trying to rescue me and take me home.

She writes her phone number on a napkin. "Call me sometime. Maybe we can go watch a Cuban movie at the Cinemateque."

We wave good-bye, and I watch her walk away. When she's out of sight, I tear the napkin with her phone number on it into pieces and stuff them in my bag.

I sit on the towel and cuddle Chispita in my

arms. "Chispitrooni, don't you worry; you're coming with me no matter where I go."

She tilts her head to the right and barks, *¡Guauuu!* Chispi always understands what I'm saying.

I pack up and walk toward the road. I stop in front of a pay phone, stick some change in the slot, and dial Marlena's number. Her grandmother answers and says in Spanish, "Marlenita and the family went to pick up her boyfriend, Ricardo, at the airport."

I gulp hard. What a great surprise. Why couldn't Marlena have told me? I guess she'd know I'd be hurt and she didn't want to spoil our time together.

We chitchat and say our good-byes. I feel as if a train just hit me. Why the heck did Ricardo have to come today of all days? Damn!

Ricardo is an eighteen-year-old guy Marlena met at her uncle Paco's house two years ago. He lives in Puerto Rico all year round with his dad. He visits his mom and Marlena whenever he can take off a week or two from work, and on holidays. Marlena has to act as if she's into him so her family doesn't get suspicious. That's messed up. Her uncle Paco, Marlena's dad, and Ricardo's dad are close friends. They want Marlena and Ricardo to get married one day. Just my luck!

I walk to the mailbox a few blocks away, get a pen and paper from inside my shoulder bag, and write Pedri a note:

> *Hi, Little Punk. I love you more than all the raindrops that have ever fallen on earth. Don't worry about me. I'll be OK. I want you to be a little man and behave. Don't get into trouble. I miss you SO much, Pedri. I'll call you every day. I love you with all my heart!*
>
> *Ten kissies on the tip of your nose!*
> *I love you, love you, love you!*
>
> > *Your big sis,*
> > *Laury*

I run to the nearest drugstore and buy envelopes and stamps. I kiss the envelope and throw the letter in the mailbox.

I bolt into a jog, with Chispita on her leash. Fast red cars zoom around like flying candy. Billboards selling perfume and jewelry are everywhere.

We run a few minutes in the blazing heat, away from traffic. Every step I take, I take in the direction of nowhere. It's really hot, and my legs feel like taffy; but I keep running as fast as I can.

I've run into someone's backyard. I look up and find myself in front of a massive San Lázaro statue encased in a shrine. He's standing with a golden cane and a few dogs licking his wounds. The cane turns an aqua blue. I shut my eyes; and when I open them wide, San Lázaro is walking across the yard, talking to himself. I run after him.

"Please, please, San Lázaro, you've got to help me!"

He stops abruptly and turns to face me. I bump into him and fall to the ground. He stretches out his hand and I grab it as he pulls me up with the strength of fifty men. His eyes meet mine.

"*Muchachita.*" The man speaks to me in

Spanish. I shut my eyes and open them many times until the blurring subsides. In front of me is a little old man with a cane. I look to my right, and San Lázaro is still encased in his shrine. "You must have fainted from the heat." He helps me up. "It's a hundred and two degrees out. Let's go inside where there's air-conditioning."

He takes me indoors and gives me an icy-cold Ironber soda to drink.

He asks me what happened. As I sit on his couch, I can't hold in my pain. "My mother doesn't love me anymore. She kicked me out of the house." I sob.

"Oh, my goodness." He taps my shoulder with his hand. "That is terrible news. Mothers are very emotional sometimes."

I wipe my tears with my forearm. "It hurts so much." All the emotions I've been feeling surface.

He takes a seat next to me. "It must be very painful. I'm so sorry," he says with kind eyes. "Is there anything I can do for you? How can I help?"

I dab my tears with a napkin. "Can my puppy

get some water, and may I please use your phone?"

"Why, of course." He pats my shoulder. "Come right into the kitchen and use our telephone."

I sip my soda as he gives Chispita water in a bowl. Then I call Soli and tell her I need a place to crash. Soli doesn't wait for me to finish my explanation.

"Stay put! I'll be there in three seconds!"

That's one thing about Soli: she's never let me down.

Tongue Tango

oli honks. I kiss the *viejito* good-bye, thank him, and run to her primitive, freshly painted red VW bug.

"Holy friggin' cow!" I open the door and plop on the passenger seat with Chispita.

Soli has undergone a wild makeover. A silver ring is stuck to one nostril of her thick nose. Tiny, pitch-black dreadlocks—which she dyed blond at the tips—stand on their ends, as if they just had an electric shock. Her glow-in-the-dark cherry lipstick, neon raspberry minidress, and orange high-heeled shoes are so bright, I think I might need to put on sunglasses.

She sticks out a pierced, swollen tongue. "I'm

celebratin' our last day of school. I'm divine, aren't I?"

"Holy bananas!" I cover my eyes. "Yuck." I get weak in the knees and beg her, "Never show me again, and hide it from your mom."

She slaps my cheek. "Right. Like I'm gonna hide my tongue from Mima." She puts her foot to the pedal and *off* we go!

"What a screwed-up day, Looly. Fart Face didn't want to let us leave till we told her who wrote that letter. She thinks it's me." She lets out a wacko laugh. "I let her know, 'It's not me; but if I knew who it was, no way would I ever tell *you*, or any teacher in this *disgusting* school.' I picked up my book bag and flew out the door."

"Damn, Soli, you're way cool." I lean over and kiss her cheek. She's the greatest friend *ever*.

"I don't give a crap what they say. I'm not going back there next year anyways. I'm transferring to Miami High. You're coming with me."

"Nope. I'm quitting school."

We yap about "the Incident." I tell her every single thing that happened after Fart Face dragged me out of class.

"Those nuns are outta control. They need a good roll in the sizzlin' sack." Abruptly, Soli says something that surprises me. "I told Mima about you and Marlena."

"What?" I spring up on my seat. "Are you *nuts*? You don't tell old people about that stuff. She's gonna think I'm some sicko who checks out girls' boobs or something."

Leave it to Soli to tell her mom I'm a homo when I'm trying my best to make others believe I'm not. Just because I fell in love with Marlena, maybe she'll think I'm a big dyke, like those butch macho truck drivers.

I tremble inside to think Soli will tell other people I know. "Chill." She twirls a teeny dread-lock around her index finger. "I told her the day I caught you guys doing the Tongue Tango, almost a year ago."

"Holy pube!" I cover my face with my hands. "Your mom's known *all* this time?"

"Take it easy, bro. You know she's fly cuz of her belief in metaphysics. She's not gonna treat

55

you bad." She lifts her pencil-thin right eyebrow. "She loves you like hell even if you *are* a homo."

"I'm no homo. I'm just in love with Marlena."

Soli doesn't get it. I don't know *any*thing about homos, and I don't live that lifestyle. She thinks me loving Marlena stamps me as a lesbo for life. I hate labels anyway. I want to be free to be myself without being branded. I'm not a cow. I'm a human being.

"Right! You're not a homo, and I'm not black."

I jam up the radio, squeeze Chispita to me, turn my head away from her, and stare at the cars rushing by us.

She lowers the music and tells me *every*thing that happened after I walked out of the classroom.

"Some kids didn't care." She names five people in our class. "They told me to say hi to you. But some were really disgusted. You'd think you were a murderer."

I sigh deeply. "You think Yasi, Aracelis, and Cecilia will always hate me?" These were my good friends at school since first grade. I dread the response.

"They were the *worst*. They said they'd rather lick scum off toilets than ever be your friend again. They're pissed you lied. But if you *had* told them, they'd have stopped being your friend anyway. So what's the difference? They're *id*iots."

Soli thinks she's helping me by telling me the truth. I kinda wish she'd shut her fat trap. My heart is feeling something heavy.

"Don't worry, Looly. You've got *me*. Who cares about those stupid thugs anyways."

She asks me to tell her every gory detail about what happened with Mami. I let it spill.

"Your mom's a nutcase." She slaps my cheek. "You'll be all right, bro. You're staying with us. Don't you worry. Mima and me love you to death."

I love Soli to death and back to resurrection, too. I guess I'm lucky to have a best friend I'm tight with.

Soli dumps me in her front yard and yells to her mom, "Mima, Looly's in bad shape!"

Viva runs to me, picks me up by the waist, and swings me around. "Laurita!" Her eyes light up so much, it makes her pastel pink, polyester housedress look even brighter. She doesn't make me feel ashamed or embarrassed, or like I'm some circus freak, like Mami, Fart Face, and my ex friends think. So I try to act normal and give her a bunch of *besitos* on her cheek.

Soli kisses Chispita's head before letting her loose from the front seat. Chispi runs full speed to me, as if I were a steak on the loose.

"Later, gators!" Soli waves good-bye. She booked just two people for haircuts today, and she's going to work early. She works cutting hair at Heads Up, where she meets more guys than most people have hair on their head.

I carry Chispita in my arms so she doesn't run after Soli's car. I sing to her, "Chispitrini Miniweeni wore a size-three bikini. I took her to the beach, now she thinks she's a genie!"

She licks my face as if I were a snow cone.

"Chispita is full of sand, Laurita. You need to take her a bath." Viva pushes my hair away from my face and kisses my forehead. "Soli tell me what happen." Her tiny, slanted eyes show concern. "I is so sorry, *mijita*. Your mami and those nuns has a lot to learn in this life. Your mami will come around." She looks right into my eyes. "You and Chispita is welcome to stay here until your mami lets you back. And if she no let you back home, you stay here forever."

I let out a long sigh of relief.

"But you must keep in touch with your mami and tell her where you is living. Keep tings organized and take care of Chispita so she no ruin nothing. She cannot do *caca* or *pipí* in the duplex. Okay?"

I kiss her *café*-colored cheeks. "Thanks, Vivalini. I'll organize every day. And don't worry. I've trained Chispi not to poop or pee indoors."

I place my little mud ball on the ground, and she runs after a lizard.

Viva starts in about how I need to register at another school right away and finish my education.

"I'd rather pierce my eyeballs and get a tattoo

of Sai Mu on my nose than go back to school."
Sai Mu is a swami guru Viva's in love with, but
she won't admit it. I try to be funny, just to get
out the pain that's stuck inside me.

"*Ay*, Laurita." She lets out a sweet laugh, like
a lullaby.

I dash through the front doors and pass Viva's
shrine to Sai Mu on my left, surrounded by man-
goes, bananas, tangerines, stones, and leaves. The
duplex smells fruity fresh.

Viva scoops up my little fleabag and follows
me indoors. I call Soli's cell and tell her to pick up
my things from behind the bush after work.

Viva left to clean someone's house—what she
does for a living—as I was scrubbing Chispita
clean. Finally I'm showering.

Boonga-boom-boom! I can tell it's Soli banging on the front door. She's got a key, so I know
she's knocking just to bother me.

Chispita rushes to the door and barks up a
storm.

"I'm coming! I'm coming!" I dry off in Soli's

room and scramble around in my bag for my cotton stretch shorts and green, holey, sleeveless T-shirt. I slip on my Swedish clogs, jump over piles of Soli's clothes, get to the living room, and swing open the door.

Soli bolts through the door. Without cracking my usual smile, I say, "Wasss up, Hootchi Momma?"

"*You're* up, bro! And I'm not gonna let you get bummed!" She picks me up, throws me over her shoulder, drops me on the flowered peach-and-orange couch, and holds down my wrists.

I struggle to get out from under her. "Get *off* me!" She's got me pinned down good and has started to tickle my stomach. Twisting and turning, I howl, "Stop!"

"See, I win every time, ha!" She smiles triumphantly. She takes my face in both of her hands, presses her lips to my forehead, and kisses me with her usual loud *muuua!* "Eat your Wheaties for breakfast and spinach for dinner, you big wussy. You ain't nothin' but a wimpy femmy lesbo."

61

I can't help but chuckle.

I unexpectedly pinch her left boob, and she lets out a ballistic laugh. I push her off me and rake my dripping wet hair back with all my fingers. I pass the arched entrance into the bright orange kitchen, filled with spider plants and hanging copper pots.

I hear Soli scream to someone outside, "Come in!" She always leaves friends waiting in the car.

A scrawny, gringo-looking guy with straw-colored hair and long arms and legs follows Soli into the kitchen. "Looly, this is Lewis."

"Hey." We kiss each other hello. He stands against a wall with arms crossed over his chest. He reminds me of a lamppost.

I pour ground Café Bustelo into the coffee-maker.

"Looly's a trip." Soli's called me Looly ever since we were in second grade. "She loves to paint, she can't live without nerdy romantic music, and she turns old men's checkered polyester golfing pants into miniskirts and bandannas. She's a Green Party member, and she visits homeless and sick kids at shelters. She's anti-chemicals, antipollution, antipesticides, and she's a veggie," she tells El Gringo, as if he gave a royal raccoon's whisker.

"Yeah. How would *you* like it if people roasted *you* and had *you* for dinner, Butt Face?" I say.

Soli kisses El Gringo's lips. "I wouldn't mind Lewis roasting me up good and taking a few bites outta me."

El Gringo gives a cute, crooked smile. I laugh. They really do deserve each other.

I prepare *café con leches*. The smell of freshly brewed percolated espresso fills the duplex. Soli takes a huge sip and adds more espresso to her cup. "Dark is better." She's talking about her chocolate-colored skin. She laughs outta control, slaps her right thigh, and lifts her left eyebrow.

El Gringo's face beams brighter than a flash-light. I can tell he's fallen into her trap.

They sit on the living-room floor as I grab one of my ancient CDs from my shoulder bag on the couch. I put on my favorite song, *ever*: "The Girl from Ipanema," performed by Astrud

Gilberto and Stan Getz.

I go to the fridge, take out a box of *churros,* and throw it on the coffee table. I always feel at home when I'm here.

Soli rips open the box. "*¡Grrrr . . . Qué rico!*" She sticks a *churro* in her colossal mouth and nudges El Gringo in his skinny ribs as she crunches away. "I told you she'd put on geeky, three-hundred-year-old music, didn't I?"

El Gringo grins, and his cute, crooked teeth stick out. "Where did you and Soli meet?" he asks. His eyes dart around, checking out the wall-to-wall, plastic-framed paintings of saints; the colorful saint figurines; the tall, plastic banana plants; the mural I drew two years ago of the ocean; and the plastic, pink-chandeliered lamps.

We answer at the same time, "La Virgencita de Guadalupe Elementary, the worst Catholic grammar school in the history of the universe!" We laugh like nut balls and give each other a bunch of knuckle-to-knuckle punches.

I dunk a *churro* in my *café con leche*, stick it in my mouth, and munch on it. "We met in first grade. Soli was the only black kid in school, and no one would play with her. We played at recess and had a blast."

She kisses my cheek and smiles proudly. "Looly's my best friend."

"It's good you had Laura for a friend." El Gringo sips his *café con leche* slowly, as if he's scared of finding a goldfish or something in it.

Soli dives in. "Looly just got thrown out of school *and* her crib." She explains the reason why Mami kicked me out, and my stomach starts to burn something terrible. El Gringo listens calmly.

I feel naked as she yaps about my life. She knows I have to know and trust someone deeply before I tell people my private, personal things. I don't know what's gotten into her.

El Gringo doesn't even bat an eyelash. "No big deal. I don't care if you're lesbian. My little brother was a T-girl, you know, a transvestite."

He wants to tell us a "long story." Soli and I prick up our ears.

"Last year on spring break I went to Queendom Come Comedy, a teen street drag show in Key West, with my brother Joaquin. He performed as 'Tatiana Titi.'"

Soli and I burst out laughing.

"Tatiana Titi and his gag tranny partner, Tunisia Temper Tantrum, dressed in outrageously colorful feathered outfits and tall, fat wigs. They performed the funniest comedy act you've ever seen. The crowds were in stitches, until Joaquin changed clothes and transformed into Joy." He looks away from us, then down to the floor. "The audience became dead silent when Joy sang a love song whose lyrics she wrote." He pauses. "I say 'she' out of respect," he goes on. "She got the biggest standing ovation. I jumped on the stage and hugged her so hard. I . . . I . . ." He stutters, and his eyes well up. "I just wanted her to know I loved her no matter what."

I start tearing up.

He clears his voice. "That night my dad, who was staying at his girlfriend's place for the weekend, came home unexpectedly. He caught Joaquin in bed, under the covers, dressed as Joy. She was fooling around with Ernesto, her first boyfriend."

I widen my eyes. "What happened?"

"He beat Ernesto to a pulp, and he hit Joy so hard with his bare fists that he knocked her two front teeth out."

"No!" Soli and I shout at the same time.

"After my dad threw Joy out of the house, she moved in with a tranny friend, Noelis. Joy started doing serious drag shows." He throws out a sweet smile. "As a kid, when our parents were away, Joaquin would sneak into our mom's closet and come out as Joy, wearing lipstick, high heels, and dresses. He was born in the wrong body. Joaquin should have been a girl." He looks down at his long, skinny fingers with the saddest eyes I've ever seen. "One night Joy went back home dressed as a boy, as Joaquin. He asked my father to forgive him. He said if he'd take him back, he'd never dress as a girl again. My dad belted him till he bled. He told him he didn't love him and he never wanted to see him again. My brother committed suicide that night."

I shudder and put my hand on his shoulder. "Oh, no. That's terrible."

A deep silence fills the room for a really long time.

He abruptly changes the subject. "What high school will you be transferring to?"

"I'm quitting school forever." I take a slurp of hot *café con leche*; it goes down smooth. "And you?"

"After Joy died, I told my dad if he didn't transfer me to Delphi High, I'd go live with my mom in Oregon."

We talk about El Gringo's life till Soli spins the focus back on me. "I can't believe Fart Face read your letter to the class." She takes a few loud slurps of *café con leche* and then bites into a *churro,* and the sugar crystals shower the floor. Chispita licks the floor clean.

"Yeah. That sucks." El Gringo can't be fazed by anything gay, which is amazing. "Lesbians are just like everyone else. There are tons of 'out' lesbians at Delphi High."

I can't relate to being called lesbian, but I won't make any waves. "Don't they treat gays terrible there?"

"No, man. It's an expensive private school for intellectually gifted and nonignorant genius kids." He goofs off and throws us a suave smile. "Like *moi*."

"Looly's wicked-smart. Wish she could afford to go there."

"Yeah. They even have LGBTQ support groups—you know, lesbian, gay, bisexual, transgender, and queer. There's also a gay-straight alliance." His expression turns droopy. "I wish Joy had gone there."

I really like this guy. He's a person with a heart. I feel like opening up to him a little.

"I could have been executed in cold blood today, in front of everybody, and I'm sure the nuns and students would have thrown a party. Some of the kids at our school for sure would set fire to a gay support group."

El Gringo wipes his line-of-a-lip with a napkin. "Delphi High is an all-American school, man. It's cuz you were at a Latino Catholic school. Man, some Cubans suck so bad, like my dad. My mom is Cuban too, but she's totally cool. My dad's just like all the right-wing extremist assholes of the world. He hates gays and blacks and the environmentalists and shit like that." He shakes his head. "He's twisted, man. I can't wait till I turn eighteen and can move out. I never want to be like him. He and those nuns are ignorant fools. You and Joy are a million steps above them all."

For the first time ever I don't feel like saying I'm not gay. I almost feel gay inside. I mean, I don't know the difference between those lesbo girls at the gay beach and me except that they're "out." I don't know. It's a weird-ass feeling. Maybe I *am* gay and I just won't admit it.

Soli changes the conversation. She always does just when things start getting juicy. She hates talking politics, or anything serious, for too long. She says, "It cramps my style, bro."

"Hey, tell Lewis how I used to wear pigtails in elementary school."

I pull my little tick machine to me and squeeze the furry ball into my arms. Soli's trying to entertain me. I can tell she knows I'm going through hell and wants to make me laugh. I don't want her to feel bad. So I start: "She always had three pigtails, two on the sides and one on top of her head. She looked like she was sprouting trees."

"Hey!" She slaps my cheek. "I was *way* fly for my time."

"Right!" I pinch the tip of her nose. Chispi barks at her in agreement. "Her mom starched and ironed her dresses every morning. Her uniform was stiff as a board."

Soli tosses her head back, opens her mouth so wide you can see her tonsils, and lets out an ear-splitting laugh. Her eyes light up. "Bro, remember how Sister María de los Ángeles used to grab your cheeks and pinch them hard when you were sketching instead of paying attention in class? Remember the day Sister Petra cut your shaggy hair in class and gave you short bangs cuz she said she couldn't see your eyes?"

"What a freak!" I crack up laughing.

She faces El Gringo. "In third grade, this girl Olga once yelled to me, 'Slave! Black bootie bitch!' And Looly screamed to her, 'Look who's talking. You're white like dirty sour milk. At least *she* looks like yummy chocolate!'" I can't stop laughing. Soli goes on. "Another time Olga screamed to me, 'Hey, Charcoal Momma, come shine my shoes!' Looly said to me, 'Don't pay attention to her.' She pulled me by the hand, took me to the far corner of the playground, and started making jokes. She made me laugh outta control with her wacky sense of humor."

I look at the colorful friendship wristband I gave her for her birthday. I rub the one she gave me for mine, and we throw each other a smile.

One thing about Soli is that things never get to her. She's not sensitive like me. I mean, look at all the crap those kids called her; but as long as she had me, she didn't care. And she's not a neuro about it either. Nothing fazes her. All those nasty names I got called today will be stuck in my heart—like a sharp knife that gets twisted in there—for*ever*. Soli says she's never even cried about all the horrible stuff kids called her. Things just slide off her chest easily. And that's a gigantic chest, let me tell you!

I wish I could be like Soli.

Viva comes in and spreads kisses. *"¡Eh, familia!"*

"Lewis," I tell El Gringo, "this is Viviana Celina de la Risa Catalina del Carmen Cabrera Prieto de Santillanos." Viva laughs up a storm, and her chubby belly ripples. She loves that I've memorized her entire birth name.

Viva plops on the couch and fixes the little Mercurochrome-colored bun on top of her head with bobby pins. When she finds out that I haven't called Mami yet, she reprimands me. "Laurita, call your mami *now*. Tell her you is staying with me."

"Yeah, Looly, get it over and done with."

I drag my feet toward the phone. I feel my heart in the pit of my stomach as I dial Mami's number. I know I have to call her or Viva won't let me stay.

"¿Hola?" she answers in a stern voice.

"Hi, Mami." I shake inside; it feels like a razor blade is stuck in my throat.

She growls, "'Hi, Mami? Hi, Mami?'" She repeats it as if I didn't hear her the first time.

"How will a 'Hi, Mami' ever take away what you've done to our family name? You've disgraced us." I gulp knives and razor blades and bombs that explode in my stomach.

"Mami, please relax." I lie next to Viva on the couch and lay my head on her lap. She gently smooths the hair away from my face.

"Re*lax* when your own daughter gets thrown out of school, and she lies about having slept with a degenerate in this house? Is the *degenerada* Soli? Is it?"

"No, Mami. It's not Soli. I swear on Papi's grave." She knows I only swear over my father's dead body to say the truth. I close my eyes. "Mami, please, I'm in really bad shape. Please. Don't make things worse." I feel as if I'll die of a heart attack if she keeps this up.

"If Osvaldo finds out, I'll kill you!"

I go on with a trembling voice. "Viva will let me stay at her place if you don't want me anymore." This is a hint, to see if she still loves me and wants me back. I mean, if I were a mother, I'd want my kid back no matter what.

"How could I want you if you're abnormal, a liar, you've ruined my life, and you'll be a bad influence on your little brother?" I hold the receiver away from my ear. Everyone hears everything. "I've replaced the locks. You're never stepping foot in here again unless you tell me her name and until you've changed into a normal, decent human being who plans on one day getting married and having children. Otherwise, stay with those immoral people who accept degenerates." She slams down the phone.

I feel my throat tightening.

"*Ay*, Laurita." Viva helps me sit up. She lifts my chin with her index finger. "Your mother loves you, *mariposita*. She is just scaring you into changing."

"Looly, don't worry. Your mom's a freak. You've got us."

El Gringo jumps in. "Your mom's the one with the problem, Laura, not you."

Soli tells Viva about Joy. Viva's eyes show concern. "We love you *mucho, mucho*, Laurita. Tings will be better. You will see. I is going to buy you a bike. No need to get yours at your mami's."

Viva takes a *merenguito* from her dress pocket and hands it to me.

I don't want anyone to worry about me or think that maybe I'll commit suicide like Joy, so I act goofy. "Yummy!" I say. "White plastic sugar!" I lift it in the air. "*Merenguitos,* nothing can be better for a quick diabetic coma!"

Chispita takes a flying leap and almost grabs the *merenguito* from my hand. The right side of Viva's lips lifts way up high as she laughs. She holds my hand like only a mother can. She kisses my right cheek, and Soli kisses my left cheek. I think that maybe, just maybe, I'll live through all this.

Yours and Only Yours

For the past two months it's been a blast living at Soli's. I'm sleeping on the living-room pull-out couch and it's supercomfy. Soli and I go to the movies or the beach boardwalk a lot. I help Viva clean, wash clothes, organize, and cook. I give her rent and food money, but no way will she take it. She makes me save it in the bank. Mami still won't let me back unless I spill the *frijoles*, but at least I get to talk to Pedri every day. He sneaks calls to me when Mami's taking a bath.

I started working full-time with Marlena's uncle Paco. Some days after work I throw my bike in the back of Paco's truck and we head on over to his house—he always invites me to eat. I bathe and then chill with Marlena. We make love when the house is empty. Soli always picks me up. I put my bike on her car's bike rack, and she takes me home.

Ricardo stayed in Miami for two weeks. Marlena and I were bummed. She had to see him every day. The good thing was that she snuck phone calls to me every second she wasn't with him. And we talked every night before going to sleep.

The terrible news, though, is that last week Marlena's brother left early to go back to Puerto Rico because of an emergency with his girlfriend. As soon as he arrived, her dad called. He said that Marlena wouldn't be finishing high school in Miami as he had promised her. He'd already enrolled her in Academia Biblia, a Bible academy high school. Now she has to return to Puerto Rico right away to start school next week. Her family misses her and wants her home.

● ● ●

Marlena's *tío* Paco, *tía* Hilda, *abuelita,* and little nieces help Marlena carry her bags into the taxi. We kiss everyone good-bye and climb into the backseat.

A bearded Cuban guy with a hairy chest and bushy arms remarks, *"No hablo inglés."*

He doesn't speak English, and that's way fly with us. He puffs on his big, fat cigar. Disgusting smoke ringlets float up to the ceiling.

We roll down our windows, and I throw my head out for fresh air. I look past the expressway, toward the shoreline filled with neon-colored apartment buildings. Marlena's uncle's house is getting smaller and smaller in the distance, and my heart sinks.

I look at Marlena. "I can't believe you're leaving."

"Don't worry. After my eighteenth birthday, I'll come here for work. I promise." She whispers, "Nothing will ever separate us."

"Jesus." I roll my eyes. "That's six hundred years from now."

"Huy, Scrunchy. It's a year and seven months

away." She looks away from me and stares out the window.

I scoot down to where Hairy Taxi Guy can't see me and whisper to her, "Okay, okay. I'll wait for you till my teeth fall out and I turn into a wrinkly prune."

A bunch of gay guys pass us in a Jeep, blasting disco music. They're holding hands and having fun, as if they just don't care. They don't seem scared. I'm sure they're not Cuban.

Hairy Taxi Guy throws them a bird. *"¡Maricones de mierda!"*

I slouch down with my knees up on the back of the passenger seat and whisper, "What a prince."

Marlena looks into the rearview mirror to make sure Hairy Taxi Guy isn't looking at us or trying to understand our conversation. "I guess people knowing you're like *that*"—she snaps her fingers and her bracelets *clink, clink, clank* all the way down to her elbow—"is everyone's worst nightmare. Everybody hates people who act like *that*."

She lifts up her hair from her neck, lets it loose, and down it comes in a cascade of curls. I take a good look at her and my world spins. I won't see her beautiful face for almost two years!

I grab my sketchbook from my shoulder bag. "I'm going to sketch you one last time. I won't be able to do it again till *la luna* turns purple."

She throws me one of her smiles that is so warm, so tender. I wish I could stick it in my pocket so I could keep it forever. "Great." Her eyeballs roll over to Hairy Taxi Guy, then to me. "But just act normal."

I knock off my sandals, remove my seat belt, lean my back against the door, and put my feet on her plump thighs. Now I have a reason to stare at her without Hairy Taxi Guy thinking I'm a weirdo homo.

I outline her profile with my charcoal pencil: her sunken eyes; a nose that broke when she fell off trying to ride a bike; the delicate shape of her lips; her round chin, short neck, and big puff of hair. I fill in details: her cheekbones pop out; her hair becomes wild, tumbling locks; her thick eyebrows and long, spidery lashes come alive in smudges of wavy browns. I even catch the way she's looking away, so Hairy Taxi Guy doesn't get any ideas.

I take my colored pencils and color in everything. I've drawn pure love.

I pat her thigh with my foot. She looks my way, and I show her the sketch. She throws me a sweet grin.

Traffic is thrashing by. Cars are zooming from lane to lane, swerving fast in front of us.

I cross my arms over my chest and eye Marlena suspiciously. "Why did you tell me last night that I can't come visit you?" I'm bummed that she won't let me visit.

She leans against the car door and sticks her elbow out through the window. I think she's hiding something from me. Lately, since her brother Arturo left, it's as if she's got this major secret inside her; but she won't talk about what's bothering her, no matter how much I ask.

Minutes pass and she doesn't say a word. It's so quiet, you could hear a mosquito pee.

"You know Papi won't let anyone sleep over. He'll drive us nuts talking religious stuff. He won't leave us alone a second to have fun. We won't have a minute of privacy." She sighs. "I don't want to talk about it now; it's too stressful."

I let it slide. I know she's in as much pain as me. I can feel it.

A song comes on about Juana Palangana— Bedpan Juana—who looks like a banana. I can't bear seeing my Marlena so sad. I try to make her laugh and rotate my bootie in my seat, snap my fingers, and make drum sounds with my mouth, *"Gún-dún-dún-gún!"*

She cracks a loving smile.

"Hey." I jut my chin in the direction of her fingers and whisper lightly, "Are those *my* fingers?"

She wiggles her fingers, throws me a shining smile, and whispers as low as if we were in church, "They're all yours."

"If they're *all* mine, then I want them to stay *here* with me. Don't take them back to Puerto Rico, Pooki, please."

She looks down at her small, soft hands with a wilted expression.

I know what she's feeling. I know she doesn't want to leave, but she has to. I guess me bugging her to stay is like rubbing vinegar on a cut. But still, I hate that she hasn't found a single way for us to see each other. And she didn't fight to stay either, like she did last time.

We're inching our way through Little Havana's Calle Ocho's Parque del Dominó, where tons of men are playing dominoes and drinking *cafecitos*. The sugary smells of *guarapo* and *mamey* shakes seep into the taxi.

"Castro, that bastard!" a round-bellied man screams in Spanish to a shriveled-up *viejito*. The little old man looks like a heap of leather under a sombrero. Loud domino sounds slap around the tables.

Now I say something that's been on my mind. I don't like talking about things that bother me right away. I let them simmer till they're just about to explode inside me.

"Pooki, please don't keep dating Ricardo. You

know he's in love with you."

I'd never in a million years date a guy while being with Marlena. I feel hurt just knowing he's back in Puerto Rico, probably waiting for her to arrive.

Her look turns so intense, it practically throws me off my seat. "You know I'll have to date Ricardo. If I don't date him, my family will become suspicious." I see a lot of pain in her face. "You know I'm in love with you and only you. I'll love you forever. There's nothing to worry about."

Right. Like I shouldn't worry about Rick the Dick being desperate to get into Marlena's pants. He knows he won't get any unless they're married, so I know he's probably going to pop the question soon. Marlena doesn't think ahead like I do. She's just playing with fire.

She keeps yapping away about why she has to date the damned guy.

"Well, have a blast with Ricardo. Maybe I'll go out with Mauricio, a friend of Soli's who thinks I'm interesting *and* sizzlin'." I want to see if she gets jealous.

"Really?" I guess I caught her attention.

"Yeah. He's an awesome long-haired guitarist who writes his own lyrics and travels the world doing odd jobs. And he does volunteer work for the sick and homeless." She knows that would be my type of person.

She coughs and clears her throat. "Well, that's great."

"Great?" This isn't the response I want from the love of my life.

She whispers something barely audible. "Go out with him. Dating a guy is normal. Make him your boyfriend so your mom will let you back home." She sounds like a different person. "Try being his girlfriend; it's not a big deal. It's so easy. Everyone will think you like him, and they won't give you a hard time."

Out of nowhere she sighs deeply and changes the topic. "There's something I haven't told you."

"What?" I sit up straight and face her.

"My brother found my diary. That's why he left

a week early. He took it with him to Puerto Rico."

I feel my heart pounding in my chest. "Why didn't you tell me?"

"I didn't want to spoil our last days. I didn't want you to suffer like I was suffering. You've been through enough."

I look out the window at the whirling gray streets, wondering if this craziness will ever stop.

"Arturo promised he wouldn't tell anyone if I stopped seeing you."

I feel a glimmer of hope in my heart. "You lied and promised, right?"

"Yes, but he left a message on my cell this morning that he's changed his mind. He's going to tell my parents but no one else." She closes her eyes as if in prayer. "I tried calling him back, but he wouldn't answer the phone."

"Shit. How can we make him stop?"

"It's not in our control."

"I hope he never tells your uncle Paco."

"Don't worry. He won't. Arturo said the more people know, the more my name will be smeared. He says he'll beat me up if I get a bad reputation and Ricardo finds out."

"He better not touch you."

I feel scared for Marlena. Her brother gets violent when he's angry. When she was little, if she misbehaved, he'd belt her really hard till he left welts on her.

"There's nothing we can do. We've lost. Everyone is against us. I wish I'd never written that letter to you. I wish I'd never written a single word about us in my diary."

"We haven't lost if we still love each other."

She speaks in a sad, low tone. "We're doomed. We'll never be able to see each other again. Arturo said Papi is going to stop paying for my cell phone."

"We've got e-mail." She sounds weird, as if she wants to give up on us.

"Arturo is changing our home phone number. He's making Papi stop paying for my e-mail service too; he's gone crazy. We won't be able to contact each other anymore."

I shut my eyes really hard and rub them. "You can e-mail me from the library." I'm trying to find quick solutions. "We can IM every day. I'll save money and buy you a BlackBerry."

She takes a huge gulp and whispers so low that I have to force myself to listen. "They'll search me and find it. I can't deal with this. It's too hard. I'm not strong like you."

"Please. Please, don't talk like that." I stare out the window at the fluffy clouds. They always soothe me, but it's not working right now. I glance back at her. "Listen, just lie and promise your parents you'll never communicate with me for as long as you live." I rub my face with my hand. "Tell them their God and Jesus are all about loving people like prostitutes and sinners. Tell them that if Jesus forgave Mary Magdalene, they can forgive you."

"Oh, Laura." Her seriousness makes my hands shake. "Arturo read me parts of my diary where I talk about how much I love kissing your entire naked body . . . and the way you . . . we . . ." She doesn't finish her sentence and takes a deep breath. "He said he's going to read every detail to my parents. Can you believe it?"

"What a sicko." I can't believe he'd do something so horrible.

"Everything's changed. Nothing will ever be the same. I'm sorry I didn't tell you about the diary sooner." She looks gently into my eyes. "How can we stay together with them knowing and without things getting worse?"

"Just stay. Don't go back." I rub my forehead. I'm getting a big, fat headache. "Don't board that plane. We'll figure out a place for you to live."

"I can't do that. Arturo will come find me. He'll kill me." I see sadness etched across her face. "I'm trapped." She wrings her hands. "I know Papi and Arturo will hound me twenty-four hours a day now."

I look away from her. How could she not want to find ways to ever see me or talk to me again? What's gotten into her?

"You're breaking it off?"

"What else can we do?" Her voice is meek. I know she doesn't mean what she's saying. She's just terrified.

"We'll figure something out."

"Okay," she says, but she doesn't sound convinced.

We get to the airport, inch up the ramp, and park. "*Gracias*." Marlena pays Hairy Taxi Guy. We dart into the airport and push through the crowds; and before you know it, it's almost time.

We run to find privacy. I see a sign on a bathroom door that says "Fresh Paint. Do Not Enter." We walk in, lock the door behind us, and rush into a stall. "I love you with all my heart and soul." She caresses my hair and face with the gentlest touch in the world. "I'll miss you so much. I'll die without you."

"I love you with all my might." I hold her face in my hands and fill it with soft kisses.

"I can't wait till you come back."

Her voice cracks. "I don't think I can come back. I won't be able to handle being with you here. It'll be too stressful." She breaks down into sobs.

I lift her chin with my index finger and kiss her tears. "Please, don't ever say that."

She squeezes her cheek gently against mine. "I'm so sorry. I'm so very, very sorry, Scrunchy."

I gently glide my hands against her dark, velvety face. "We'll work it out, Pooki. Our love is powerful; it's for eternity." I kiss her cherry mouth one last time, then her closed eyelids. "Don't ever say you'll leave me."

She kisses my forehead. "Never." I feel relieved. "You're right. We'll find a way."

I squeeze her in my arms. "You'll be all right. I went through it. We'll be together forever, no matter what, right?" I need to hear an answer.

Instead, she checks the time. "Hurry! It's time!" She grabs my hand and pulls me toward the door. She swings the door open and we're bombarded by chaotic noise and throngs of people moving around. We rush toward the screening area.

We sink into a sad silence, hugging hard, holding on to each other.

She lets go of me and walks stoically through the metal detector. Tears streaming down her face, she turns to wave to me one last time and calls, "Take good care of yourself."

It sounds as if we're never going to see each other again.

I wipe the tears dripping down my cheeks, and I mouth, "I love you."

Pink Petunias

It's midnight, March 26, and Marlena's seventeenth birthday. Soli and Viva are asleep. I carry Chispita in my arms and tiptoe onto the dark back porch. I sit on Viva's rocking chair and rock back and forth, back and forth, squeezing Chispita to me. I hear thunder clap and watch thin veils of rain cover the trees.

Days have been longer without my Marlena. She left seven months and four days ago. At first she wrote me love letters every day and managed to sneak collect calls to me three times a week. As time went on, she made her family believe that I was history *and* a sinful mistake. Her online services were restored, and her e-mails and IMs poured in. Eventually she started calling me late every night and when no one was home.

I was expecting Marlena to move to Miami in June of next year. She seemed to have gathered enough courage to do so. She wouldn't move in with me for fear of others finding out and in case her family visited, but at least we'd be together. Even though Cuban and Puerto Rican girls must live at home till they get married regardless of their age, here she'd be considered an adult at eighteen. According to the law, her parents would have no say.

I planned to help her find a place nearby, pay the rent, and get a job. Then last month the calls, letters, e-mails, and IMs abruptly stopped. I've tried every possible way to contact her, but to no avail. I know she's still alive and well, because Paco mentions her often.

I've been working like a fiend and chillin' with Viva and Chispita on weeknights and holidays. Early weekend mornings, around 5:00 A.M., I pack a picnic and ride the tall-handlebar bike that

Viva bought me to Key Biscayne beach. There I walk, swim, sketch, write poetry, and think till after sunset.

Soli and I kick it on weekend nights. I got her—and whatever guy she's dating—into seeing foreign movies and chillin' at Bohemian Café on poetry nights. Unfortunately, going out makes me miss Marlena even more.

I miss her face, her gestures, her voice, and everything about her.

Now mild breezes bring the smell of the damp, green night onto the porch, but my stomach is twisting as if I'd eaten a jar of habanero peppers.

I rock back and forth, back and forth, thinking, like I've done every day since Marlena left. Life is so messed up sometimes. Just when you think everything is a bed of pink petunias, a dog comes and poops on it.

I didn't get to sleep till late last night. I'm riding my bike through woodsy Coconut Grove after work, with the cool, salty air filling my lungs.

I can't stop thinking about what happened today:

Beep, beep! *"You guys keep working. Laura is coming with me!"* Paco commands in his usual Spanish. *I throw down my shovel and climb into his sneaker-smelling blue Toyota pick-up truck. "We're going to the nursery warehouse to get more trees."*

He zooms off.

"I just got some great news. My brother called from Puerto Rico to tell me Marlena is getting married to Ricardo!" His eyes sparkle. "I just spoke with Marlena. She sounds happy as a fiesta!" He scratches his barrel belly and sings, "Here comes the bride, here comes the bride. . . ."

I gulp hard, turn to look at him, and put on a smiley face. "Great."

I'm snapped out of my thoughts by a red Beemer honking at me. "Get off the *foc*ing road with that *foc*ing bike! *¡Comemierda!*"

"I love you too!" I scream, and swerve over to the sidewalk before he runs me over. I get back to thinking that at least Marlena's family never told Paco on us; but that's not the way I wanted to hear about my Marlena again, thank you very much. I hope she's not really marrying Rick the Dick. That she hasn't been able to call me tells me she might be going through hell, unless she stopped giving a shit. Then *that's* a different story!

I zip on to US 1 and pass a truck burping black fumes. "Gross!" I yell to the driver while holding my nose and pointing at the guck polluting the air.

I zip to Little Havana. I let the smells of cut grass and coconut milk soothe me before I get home. I don't want to bring Chispi or Viva down and must act happy.

I park my bike and fling open the door. My furry chicken pot pie leaps onto me. "How's my little miniscloopi, the cutest macarooni in the world, eh?" I scoop her up and cover her with smoocheroonies. She licks my eyelids and nose.

Viva stops brushing the ceiling with a sopping wet broom full of the nontoxic cleaners I bought her. She kisses my cheek. *"Hola, mijita."* She takes out a pink tissue from inside her bra and dusts the drooping crystals on her plastic chandelier. "How is *la mariposita* today?"

"I is so fine I shine," I say, goofing, trying hard to hide my feelings. "Don't forget that spot." I point to another corner of the ceiling. "Who knows *what* bacteria's growing there." Viva is a psycho cleaner.

"Ay, Laurita." She laughs as sweet as guava cream.

I dash to the computer to see if Marlena left an e-mail. No such luck.

I rush to use the phone as Viva leaves to buy Chispita Milk-Bones at the corner *mercado*. On her way home she'll stop at her best friend Adela's apartment for a *cafecito* and a long yack about Sai Mu, astrology, and spiritual things.

I call Pedri like I do every day after work. I don't give three flying *fricasés* if Mami keeps answering and hanging up on me.

"Little Punk!"

"Laury!" I imagine him throwing his arms around my waist and squishing his tiny head against my stomach.

He sniffles into the receiver. "Pedri, what's wrong?"

"I miss you."

It's getting harder and harder to live without my little bro. I clear my trembling voice. "Me too, Little Punk. I miss you so much I could die."

"Why don't you just sneak into the house at night to come see me?"

"Mami changed the locks a loooooong time ago. I don't have the new set of keys or I'd be there every day. But no matter what, I'll always love you." I shut my eyes. "Hey, close your eyes and think that I'm hugging you." I envision myself squeezing him to me. "I love you more than anything or anyone in this world. Can you feel that?"

"Yeah!" I can feel his smile radiating around me.

I sit on the couch and imagine him on my lap, the way he always put his head on the curve of my neck and sucked his thumb. I miss his coconut cookie smell that reminds me of home.

"Did you get the letter and pictures I sent you this week?" He told me Mami has been throwing out my mail.

"Yesterday Mami ripped up and threw away the cartoon book you made me. I cried the *whoole* day. I didn't eat or nothing last night. She promised she'll give me everything you send me from now on. I'm saving your old letters and pictures inside last year's lunch box." I always send him tons of funny pics of Chispita, Soli, Viva, and me.

"Don't worry, Little Punk. I'll make you a new book; it'll be even funnier! And I'm sending you my favorite painting of Chispita with bananas flying around her."

He gives out a sweet belly laugh. "That's funny, Laury. I can't wait. I'll put it up in my room. She's so cute. I miss her, too."

"I know." It's so unfair what Mami's doing to us.

"I can't see Chispita anymore neither. That's bad. I didn't do nothing wrong." And neither did I, I think.

I hear Mami and Osvaldo talking. I speak fast into the receiver. "I love you, Little Punk. Call me later, when she's taking a bath! I love you more than the clouds and the tallest trees, and all the flowers on Earth."

"I love you too, Laury. More than all the puppies and kitties and ponies in the world."

Click! We hang up fast so Mami doesn't catch him on the phone with me.

Mami will have to cut off my fingers to stop me from calling my little bro. She'd have to chop off my legs to stop me from visiting him at school during some of my lunch breaks from work.

Just as I'm headed to go online the phone rings.

"*¿Oigo?*"

"This is a collect call from Puerto Rico. Will you accept?"

"Yes!"

"Hello?" Marlena's voice sounds distant.

"Pooki, my God!" I plop on the sofa and exhale a great sigh of relief. "It's so good to hear your voice." Words pour out fast. "Are you okay? It's been so long. Paco told me you're getting married. Why did you stop calling me? What happened?" I'm jittery and out of breath. "How are you? You're not really marrying Ricardo, are you?"

"Hi, Laura. I'm fine." She doesn't call me Scrunchy. Her voice sounds odd, not the voice of someone psyched to talk to me. "I got really busy and haven't been able to sneak another call till now."

"How are things at home? What's happened since we last talked?" I can't stop asking questions. "Paco talks about you a lot. Are you being forced to marry Ricardo? It must be so hard."

"No. I'm not being obligated to do anything. Everything's great at home because I've changed."

She doesn't sound like my old Marlena; she's someone I don't recognize.

"You mean you've changed because you're acting like you're in love with Ricardo, right? But you're not going through with the marriage, right?" With all my heart I want to hear that she still loves me, she's coming back to live in Miami as we'd planned, and she's not marrying Rick the Dick, no matter what.

"No. I mean I've really changed, Laura. Papi put me in advanced nightly Bible study classes last month. I'm learning the New Testament at a much deeper level than I do at school. What we were doing was wrong." She speaks in a dead tone, as if she were talking about dust on her counter, as if our two years and eight months together—not counting last month—didn't mean a thing. "I don't want to be a sinner anymore."

"A sinner? Are you *crazy*? What have they done to you?"

She continues after an awkward silence. "Please, don't make it difficult for Ricardo and me. We're getting married next Sunday, and we're flying off for our honeymoon to Santo Domingo."

"Is *this* what you're calling me for, to kick me

in the stomach?"

I hear her make a strange moan. "I called to let you know I've moved on with my life, and I can't be like that with you anymore."

I grab Chispita and place her on my lap for comfort. "But being like *that* was the happiest time of our lives."

"It's indecent and immoral; it's not normal." Someone took my Marlena and replaced her with a robot.

"You're sounding wacko, like my mom and the nuns and the kids that called me names." I sigh. "I don't know what's gotten into you. You're killing me. It's your crazy brother and dad's fault. You're letting them force you into believing that what we did was evil."

"No, Laura." She pauses for a second, then goes on. "I figured that out for myself after I read the Bible."

"The Bible also talks about monsters, unicorns, angels having sex with women, and it being okay to have slaves and stone people to death. You believe in those things, too?"

She doesn't respond to my question. Instead she repeats, more serious than ever, "What we did was wrong and sinful."

Marlena has slipped away from me.

"Love isn't sinful, Marlena." I don't call her Pooki so she knows I mean business. Chispita jumps off the couch and plops on the floor. I sit next to her, grab my sketch pad and a pen from the coffee table, and start doodling. "We've known each other since we were eleven, and we were together more than two years. You *know* our love was beautiful. You *know* you loved me with all your heart." I throw the sketch pad and pen on the floor.

She clears her throat and steers the conversation in another direction. "All I can say is that I've been walking a pure path by dating Ricardo, and I've decided to accept his proposal. I want to marry Ricardo." She talks in a dry tone, without much feeling, like someone depressed. "He comes over, and we have dinner together every night with my family. We hang out and watch movies. We also go to church on Sundays together, as a family, with his family and mine. We get along great."

"Are you in love with him?" I just want to hear the whole truth.

"I'm trying to fall in love with him. I think eventually I will. He's good to me, and my family loves him."

"So you suddenly stopped loving me, right?" I close my eyes and wait for the answer.

There's a long, crazy-ass silence. She covers the receiver, and I think I hear her crying.

"I still care about you," she says carefully, in a trembling voice. "You were my closest friend. We had a lot of fun, and we went through a great deal together." She sighs really deeply. "I can never go back to the way we were."

I look out the backyard windows. Light purple streaks melt into yellows and reds. But at least they sink in vivid colors.

She coughs and clears her voice. "I need to hang up. I'm on a pay phone. Ricardo is about to get to my house, and I've been out too long. I don't want anyone getting any ideas."

I massage my eyes; they're throbbing with pain.

"Can you call me some other time so we can finish this conversation?" It's hard to believe that Marlena doesn't give a royal crap about me anymore.

"I can't. Don't you understand? It's over. I pray you have a good life. I hope you find a boyfriend who loves you as much as Ricardo loves me. Please accept this and let go. I'll pray for you so you too can change and lead a righteous life."

I'm startled by Soli's loud banging on the front door and by her shrieky singing as she walks in: "Food time! Chow time! I brought a feast for all of us, Looly, so you don't have to cook tonight." She places a large, garlic-scented bag on the kitchen table.

"Betrayer!" I yell into the receiver. I hang up the phone, throw it against a wall, and dash into the bathroom with Chispita after me. I slam the door behind me, swing it open a few times, and shut it so hard that I think I've broken it.

"Looly, what's wrong?" Soli comes to the bathroom door.

I scream out everything that happened. "She's a friggin' betrayer!"

I punch the door over and over again till my knuckles bleed. I drop to my knees. A hard pain fills my bones. I curl up into a ball on the cool terrazzo floor. Nothing matters. The sky is closing in on me.

Soli knocks on the door. "Open up, Looly!"

Chispita jumps on me to lick the blood off my knuckles and to comfort me. I place her next to me and spoon her.

Soli pleads in a calmer voice, "Please, Looly, come out."

My body shakes with pain. I stick my head in the toilet and throw up neon yellow bile—the color Mami would've loved me to paint the bathroom walls.

I wash my face, splash cold water on myself, brush my teeth, and open the door.

Soli grabs me forcefully and pulls me against her. "I *know* it's hard."

"You don't know shit!" Tears burst out of me. "No one knows what I'm going through inside. No one!"

Soli grabs my arm and pulls me into her

bedroom. She throws the piles of clothes off her bed and we climb onto it. I cuddle up into Soli's arms under her patched quilt. She smells like caramel candy, like she used to when we were little. I soften up. "You're my best friend, Soli. I love you. Please don't ever leave me."

"I'll never leave you, Looly. We're friends for life."

I hold her as tightly as I can and let the tears gush out of me.

Xed Out

Today is the Betrayer's wedding. Soli and I
tore up Marlena's letters and we burned
them. I asked her to take me to a club. I'm
determined to forget the Betrayer if it's the last
thing I do.

Soli and Diego, her newest boy toy, brought
me to Papaya's, a lesbo club. We got in thanks to
Diego, better known as DJ-Smooth, who's a part-
time DJ here and who fixed us up with false IDs.

Tazer, the boi I met at the beach the day Mami
kicked me to the curb, called Soli for a haircut,
and Soli invited her—I mean "him"—to come.
After hearing El Gringo call Joy "she," Soli and I

decided to treat Tazer as the gender he feels he really is. Soli's been buzzing and dyeing Tazer's hair for months now. I've stayed completely out of the picture and sent my hellos every now and then.

Papaya's is filled with gays, straights, bis, drag queens, and trannies, but mostly with feminine-looking lesbo, white Cuban girls. The lesbos are closeted and want to look like the straights, so they wear tons of gloppy makeup, high heels, gross perfume, and lots of gold jewelry. I look different, as if I don't belong. I threw on my tight, white corduroy hip-huggers and a white silky top that shows my belly button. I slid on my square-toed brown ankle boots and smudged a little organic mandarin lip gloss on my lips.

I'm twirling around a group of drag queens and kings. The queens start dancing around me, clapping with their hands up in the air, singing, "You go, girl! Shake it like you wanna break it!" We dance nonstop for well over an hour. I'm all sweaty, so I stop for a breather and kiss the "girls" good-bye. They say, "You're faaabulous!

Come back soon, sugar!"

Soli and Diego are in a dark corner, arms around each other, making out like a pair of horny newlyweds. She looks weird in Diego's baggy jeans and floppy shirt, my work hiking boots, and a nose ring that sticks out like a sore wart. She's trying hard to look butch, just for fun, but it doesn't work. She's more fembo than the femmiest girl in the universe.

Soli leaves Diego and comes over to me in long strides, smiling, arching her right eyebrow.

"Bro"—she fiddles with her nose ring—"dancing with queens and kings is fly, but why aren't you asking a gay girl to dance?"

I point to my left foot. "It hurts. You got a problem with *that*?"

She stands with her hands on her waist, looking down at me, pressing hard on my foot with hers. "*This* foot?"

"*¡Pendeja!*"

She steps aside and tosses her head in the direction of a group of girls. "You should be all gung ho about dancing with girls. Are you chicken?"

She doesn't allow me to respond and dives back in. "Ask a girl to dance."

She'd make a good dominatrix.

"They're all *plásticas*." Looking away from her, I place my feet on top of the little glass table with my hands clasped over my stomach.

I don't like plastic girls. I wish they had mixed clubs where girls came in ripped-up jeans and holey tank tops and talked about fun things like music, art, politics, solar energy, the environment, and cultures of the world. But I forgot when I asked Soli to bring me to a gay bar that finding a down-to-earth club in Miami would be like finding a dry spot in the middle of the ocean.

She snorts in reply, "I'll ask someone to dance with you."

I straighten my spine and stare her up and down with attitude. "Yo, I just want to listen to music for a while. Do you mind?"

"You've got to forget Marlena, bro. The only way you'll forget her is by hooking up with another girl, right away." She hoists up her pants with both hands and fiddles with her nose ring.

You'd think Soli had bull balls for lunch, she's being such an overpowering testosterone queen.

"I *have* forgotten her. She's *her*story." I wag my head from left to right. "Stop mentioning her, turd ball. What's *wrong* with you? You're wacko, man." I rub my eyes. "And her name is the Betrayer." All I need is for Soli to keep rubbing Marlena in my face. Why doesn't she just leave me alone and let me be?

She pulls a chair next to me and sits. "The damned Betrayer, okay?" She waves Diego over. He's yacking with some guys.

"Listen, psycho, as soon as I got here, memories of how Marlena and I used to dance when we were alone shook me hard." I soften up. "Marlena is the only girl I've ever danced slow with, Soli. Dancing slow with her while we kissed was the most beautiful feeling I've ever experienced in my life."

She slaps her cheek and raises both eyebrows. "Well, if *that* isn't the sweetest thing I've ever heard. Looly, my God, you're a hopeless case."

"And you? You're as sensitive as a potato

chip." My mouth feels dry. I take a sip of ice-cold virgin piña colada and it gives me the shivers. I look into her eyes. "Don't be so mean." I'm expected to forget instantly, like Soli and everyone else in the world does when they break up. I wish I weren't such a dork. Soli's right. I'm so damn sensitive.

"Bro, you've got to ask a girl on a date, tonight, before we leave. You *have* to start seeing other girls im*me*diately." She gulps her Sombrero drink and crunches a couple of ice cubes. "Take it from me. I know how it goes."

I move my legs off the table, place my feet on the chair, and bring my arms around my knees. "Right. Take it from *you*: the queen of *perfect* relationships. You've left more guys than there are people in China." I clasp my hands. "Look, bringing me here was a huge mistake. It's making me realize that I'm still in love with Marlena, and I can't fall in love with another girl. I know she was it for me."

"Bro, you've *to*tally lost it." She starts rolling her eyes this way and that.

Soli has never had a love-of-her-life, so she doesn't know what I'm going through. I wish she understood so she'd leave me alone.

Instantly I realize what will make her lay off my case.

"You're probably right. Maybe I'll tell Tazer about Marlena and ask him to introduce me to his gay girlfriends," I say, hoping she'll shut her trap. "Maybe my heart will beat outta control like it's having an orgasm when I meet one of his lesbo friends." I smile big.

"Way to go, Looly!" She slaps me a high five. "I can't *wait* till Tazer gets here."

She's all jumpy and happy like a kid at a *piñata* party.

"Hold up. I'm not sure I'm ready to tell him about me *yet*. So don't go blabbing stuff about me to Tazer till I'm ready. Okay?"

Her smile falls away. She yells to Diego again. "Git your sweet A over here, boy!"

It's his day off from DJing and he wants to chill with his boys. He's a good one for her to control. He's got a soft spot for Soli, and that spot sure isn't his ding-dong. That's the *hard* spot. I know they won't last.

Diego strolls over with a lesbo vacation pamphlet in his hands, drops with a *plop* on the chair next to Soli's, and leafs through it.

Soli plunks on his lap. "Hey, check it out!" She grabs the pamphlet from his hands.

"A lesbian cruise ship! For you and any girl in here, Looly." She jams it into my face.

I swat it away. "Shut up al*ready*."

Diego wraps both muscular arms around Soli's waist and kisses her earlobe. "Let 'er be, bird." He can tell she's bothering me. She shrugs her shoulders and leans back into Diego's strong body.

"Bro, go ask *her* to dance before Tazer arrives. You've got to try out a bunch of other girls before he introduces you to one." She already told Diego about Marlena and me, which pissed me off. But there's nothing I can do about it now. And besides, he didn't give a flying porcupine.

Soli is pointing to a dark, voluptuous girl who is sitting alone. She has hair like mine: pitch-black, straight, and down to the middle of her back. Soli knows I like feminine girls with meat on their bones. Although I'm slender because I inherited my dad's genes, I'm not into anyone who talks all day about low-carb diets and is obsessed with losing weight. Instead, I get a kick out of people who *love* to chow down, who like that they're bulky, and who eat voraciously with their hands.

Diego gently kisses the back of Soli's neck. "Chill, Soli. You're crimpin' my nerves, bird." He smiles and winks at me. I smile back. I like Diego; we get each other. Soli leans back, stretches her arms above her head, finds the tips of his hair, and plays with them. Diego's and Soli's cheeks meet as she rests the back of her head in the curve of his neck.

A tall, skinny guy with a hooked nose, mildly acne-scarred face, and long, black hair comes over to us. He's wearing tight leather pants with an open leather vest. "Hey, what's *crackin'*?" He greets Soli with a kiss. Soli tells us that he's Francisco, a straight haircutter who's into music and politics and who works with her. He comes here with his bi girl cousin on weekends to dance. They talk awhile as he takes a swig of an orange drink and says to all of us, "It's a Luscious Lesbo. Want one?"

Soli jumps in. "Me and Diego are all set." She juts her nose in my direction. "Laura's the one who needs a Luscious Lesbo, but she only drinks stuff like lemonade." I know what she's trying to say, but I hope he doesn't catch on.

Before I can say "No thanks," he calls the waitress over. "One lemonade, please."

His smile radiates. "So, what's happening in *this* corner of the world?" he asks me. I feel myself blushing. I place my feet on the floor and smile shyly, like when someone's going to take a picture and asks you to say "cheese."

Soli tugs at her nose ring and scrunches up her nose. "She's a nerd. Look at her." They scrutinize me. "She's scared of lesbos."

Soli grabs my hand and Mr. Luscious Lesbo grabs my other hand, and they pull me to the dance floor. Diego goes to chill with the DJ. The waitress finds us and hands me the lemonade. She tells Francisco, "It's on the house." He thanks her. I take a swig, and it tastes damn good. Dancing next to me, Soli whispers in my ear, "He's amazing to work with. He's cool with girls being gay."

He's intriguing in a toothpick-type way. "Maybe I'll go out with him," I tell her.

I've never given a skinny person a second look. I bet I'm prejudiced. I'm open for experimentation now that the Betrayer doesn't give a royal toad's turd about me.

"You come to a *gay* girl club and you want to chill with a *guy*?" Soli stares me up and down. "What's *wrong* with you, bro?"

"*You're* what's wrong with me, psycho. You want me to forget the friggin' Betrayer, right? Well? And besides, if the Betrayer can do it, I can do it too; and this is my chance." I just want to be left alone to do what I want without Soli in my face.

I take another swig, and before you know it, the glass is empty. Mr. Luscious Lesbo takes my glass and places it on the bar. He comes back with arms up in the air, twirling around me. I dance really close to him, and we start a body-to-body slide and grind.

"I didn't know Soli had such fly friends," he says over the thump-thumping music.

"Me neither." I grab the very ends of my hair. He closes his dreamy dark eyes, and I brush his closed lids softly with my hair.

He smiles. "You're not gay, right?"

I move away from him and twirl around him twice. I think about it for a minute, then say, "Right." I guess it's just a matter of semantics. If he had asked, "You've never been in love with a girl, right?" then *that* would be a different story. I'm not lying, so I don't feel so bad.

"Cool."

Soli's suddenly in my face, poking fun at a sixties-style dance, acting as if she were swimming, holding her nose, wiggling down as if she were going underwater. She doesn't let me get into dancing with Francisco. I whisper sharply in her ear, "I know what you're doing. Get out of my face so I can dance with him and get to know him better, okay?"

She dances way up close to me. I gently push her away. "Snap, Soli, you're such a major pain."

I take Francisco's hand and start doing super-wild go-go dances from the seventies. The girls create a circle around us and clap loudly. I'm moving my hips really sexy, causing a friggin' commotion, feeling pretty damned popular.

Francisco's eyes say it all. After the crowd disperses, we dance three straight songs.

He kisses my cheek. "I'll be right back."

Soli twirls around me until he brings me another lemonade.

He hands me the drink. "For the prettiest and sexiest dancer around." He takes me by surprise and smacks me a kiss on my lips. Suddenly our mouths lock. He makes out with me more intensely, and I swiftly remove my lips from his. Kissing him doesn't feel right; it feels nothing like it did with Marlena. I'd kissed two other guys before I'd kissed Marlena, but no one compares to her. I miss our deep, smooth, delicious kisses more than ever, but I say zip and just smile.

I gulp down the lemonade fast, to wipe the taste of his kiss off my mouth. I want to be just friends. I'm over the experiment.

Now everything around me is spinning in slow motion and I can't stop cracking up.

I can't seem to stay on my feet. Soli takes the glass from my hands and holds me up.

"What's wrong with you? You can't be drunk." She sniffs the glass. "There's no alcohol in here." She hands the glass to Francisco. Is this *really* lemonade?"

He lifts his broad eyebrows that meet in the middle, and it makes his nose and scars seem fascinating. "I hope so. Juan is bartending tonight, and he's giving me free drinks."

Soli's eyes widen. "Juan? You *know* he's hardcore into Ecstasy." She looks toward Juan, who's laughing. She turns to Francisco. "Laura doesn't do drugs, you idiot!"

Francisco explains, "But I didn't know he was spiking the drinks."

"I'm *not* high," I say, trying to do some hip-hop freestyle moves, some popping and b-girling waves in slow motion. Things around me seem to be swirling fast. I'm one with everyone here. I love everybody, and I know they love me. What a great life.

I stumble around, and Soli catches me. "Let's go outside." She pushes Francisco aside. "Get out of my face!"

"But, Soli, I'm serious. I didn't know."

"Move, *idiot*. I don't want to see your face *ever* again."

Francisco holds his hands up in the air with the glass in one of them, as if a cop had a gun to his head. "Okay. Okay." He walks away.

Soli grabs my hand and walks me outside to the patio. We sit on plastic chairs in front of a small, round table by the pool. The girls next to us are talking loudly about how rich they'll be when they become doctors, dentists, and lawyers. Yuk! I lean over to Soli and whisper, "I miss Marlena sooo much," and she freaks.

She's telling me that she wants me to hook up with one of the Cubanitas when I look up and see a familiar face. "Hey, hey, hey, Tazer the Spacer, long time no see. How's it shakin'?" I feel all wobbly, but I act superblazin'. "What choo doing here? You following me around?" I laugh like a fiend and can't stop.

"Hey, *chica*, great to see you again. Soli asked me to come." He kisses my cheek and leaves a fresh mint scent around me. Suddenly my lips tingle and I have an urge to kiss him.

"You look faaabulous!" I look him over once, then twice. Tazer really is great looking.

He hugs Soli and shakes Diego's hand as he's introduced. I try to stand and feel woozy. My arms are like Jell-O, and I plunk down on the seat. "What's the scoop, Taze? You in a daze? I'm Laura Flaura." My words come out funny.

Tazer laughs. He crouches and gives me a strong hug, then fixes his suspenders and punches Soli in the shoulder. "She's slammin' cute." I guess I'm the talk of the town today.

I stare at Tazer. He looks superstylish, with baggy, dark brown pants; a tight, chocolate-colored shirt; and two-tone brown-and-white fifties-style shoes. I can't take my eyes off his white suspenders.

Tazer yaps about how he's excited that his dad finally hired Paco to do the landscaping. "I forgot you'd given me his phone number. I handed it to my dad last week. He said Paco came over right away for an estimate. He's fast and inexpensive. We'll be able to see each other every day for a few weeks, Laura." The conversation spins around to the club. "I love this place; it's got the best music in town. And lots of hot babes, too."

Everyone laughs.

Diego beams. "I'm one of the part-time DJs."

"That's ill, dawg. Sick." Tazer goofs off. I'm staring at his pinstripe bangs. The lines are turning blurry on me.

He snaps his fingers in front of my face. "Laura, *chica*, you look weird. What's up?"

Soli explains. "Some ignorant I work with let his friend put an X in her lemonade. She's never done a single drug, but she'll be okay." She frowns. "She's really stoned out of her mind."

"No way I'm stoned!" I trumpet, and everyone's eyes zoom in on me.

"What an asshole. Where's the guy?" Tazer barks.

"Forget it," Diego scolds. "Pick a fight here, and your ass be in the slammer."

"Come on." Tazer grabs my hand. "Let's dance!" He pulls me up, and in a jiffy we're on the dance floor.

Tazer moves around me. He's a pretty blazin' dancer with some slick moves. I'm totally into dancing street salsa hip-hop with him.

I grab his hand. "Let's go to the ocean, *now*." I feel all sparkly inside from dancing with a boi in a gay bar. My first time! Dancing with a queer person in front of others isn't so bad. Nobody is screaming out horrible names. Nobody looks at me weird. No one seems to care. Everybody loves me. Feels damn gooooood!

"Now?"

"Yeah, so we can swim with the sharks." I crack up outta control and stumble over someone and almost fall.

Tazer picks me up in his lean, strong arms and carries me to our table. I hold on to him by his neck as he sits. I end up on his lap. Out of nowhere tears pour down my cheeks, and I can't hold them back.

"What's wrong?"

"The Betrayer . . . my ex, Mar . . . Mar . . . Mario, the love of my life. The Betrayer got married today." I'm wetting his neck with my tears.

"I'm so sorry, Laura. It'll be okay." He gently caresses my hair.

"Help me forget, please. . . ." Tears rain down from my eyes. He holds me tightly; and out of nowhere, his touch makes me quiver all over.

"I promise. I will. I'll help you, Laura. Don't worry."

Soli and Diego come back and see me curled up on Tazer's lap.

"She'll be fine," Soli says. "The X will wear off soon. She's just getting over someone."

"The Betrayer. The Betrayer . . . ," I repeat.

"She needs to get out of this loud, smoky place," Tazer insists. "I'm driving her home."

He helps me stand up. Soli takes me by one arm and Tazer by the other. Diego walks next to us.

I kiss Soli's cheek. "You're my best friend. I love you more than all the leaves in the world and all the grains of sand."

She pushes my hair back, away from my forehead. "Me too, Looly. You'll be all right."

Tazer kisses Soli and shakes Diego's hand good-bye, and Soli and Diego go back into the club.

My stomach feels as if I swallowed a puddle of guck. Ricardo is having sex with Marlena now. He's touching all the sacred places that used to belong only to me. She said we'd be together forever. "Forever is such a lie," I say out loud.

I plop in the passenger seat, and just as Tazer starts the engine, I throw my head out the window and puke my brains out. Tears leak out of my eyes. "I miss my little bro. Take me to see Pedri. Take me now."

"It's too late, Laura." He gets a tissue from his pocket and wipes my mouth. Then he reaches for his shoulder bag and grabs a bottle of water and makes me drink it all.

I guzzle it down and feel better.

We're driving back. The buzz-buzzing in my ears sounds like angry wasps. I slide off the ring the Betrayer gave me and throw it out the window as far as I possibly can. "Screw you!" I yell into the balmy night, remembering that Marlena has already said "I do" to Rick the Dick and has already had sex with him.

Tazer yells, "Yeah, screw you, Betrayer!"

A Tazer Seed

Yesterday, Marlena's wedding day, was a really messed-up day, and last night was just as bad. And today I have to meet Chago, Paco's partner, along with his crew, and act happy. Paco left for the week to go to the Betrayer's wedding. Tazer's dad hired Paco's company, and we're landscaping the front yard of his three-story villa.

The morning is in my face like slime, and I can't wipe it off. I'm in a sweaty daze, ready to dig holes and stick in plants, as hard and as fast as I can.

Tazer is nowhere in sight. I park my bike and

see the crew waiting for me. Everybody looks about seventeen to twenty-one. I glance up at the sun, and it hides behind a dark cloud. I don't blame it. I feel like hiding, too.

Chago tells me in Spanish, "I want you to keep an eye on the crew until I get back with more trees and mulch."

"No problem." I couldn't care less about anything right now. He could've said, "Your job today is to pour truckloads of rhinoceros poop on the plants for fertilization and swim in it," and I would have answered, "*¡Fabuloso!*"

Before he bounces, he explains what needs to be done, which sounds like, *Blih, blue-blah, bloh, blih-bleh.*

I look at his round, unshaven face and nod as he's talking. I know my job by heart.

Chago tells everyone that Paco's niece, *moi*, is in charge till he gets back. I leave a smile from ear to ear on my face, which hurts to keep plastered on, till he leaves. I guess Paco wanted Chago to lie about me being his niece so the crew wouldn't slack off.

As soon as Chago splits, a short guy who looks my age, with carrot-colored hair and green eyes, says in a husky voice, "*Hola*, dude, I'm Che," as if he were the king of the world. He slaps me a high five that makes my hand sting.

"Hey, wass up?" I throw him a smile.

He's got a tattoo of two naked girls on his left arm. Their boobs are hanging out all over the place. Just what I need so early in the morning: a freshly peeled look at life.

There's an olive-skinned girl with straight, dark hair and a pinkish skin discoloration on her right cheek. She's wearing large gold earring hoops and gold bracelets. You'd never think she'd be the type to get her hands dirty in a job like this.

She throws a shining smile my way. "Hi, I'm Camila."

"*Hola.*" I kiss her cheek. She smells divine, like orange zest. I better not look at her too long so she doesn't get any ideas about me.

I turn to the next person quickly.

A tubby girl wearing a short tank top gives me

the biggest smile of all, showing buckteeth. Her blond hair is shaved short around her head. "Hey, what's cookin'? I'm Jaylene Morenson." Her cheeks flush as if she dabbed on rouge when we weren't looking. She shakes my hand.

"What up?" I smile, but not too much so she doesn't get the wrong message.

So far there's an andro, a macho sicko guy, and a straight girl in my crew. I couldn't have wished for anything better.

Che smacks his gum and stares Jaylene up and down with elevator eyes. I can tell something weird is brewing in his swollen, cocky brain.

A tall guy speaks up. "*¡Hola!* I'm George Prios." He's got a fierce look in his eyes, as if he's ready to jump into work. He smacks the arm of the burly guy next to him. "This is my big brother, Raul. He speaks just a wee bit of English."

"*¿Qué pasa, calabaza?*" Raul's large, copper-penny eyes smile. "At home they call me El Tigre." We laugh. He's wearing all white and has thick, moppy, honey-colored hair and a dark, bushy beard. He's stocky, and he does remind me of a tiger. He extends his hand for a strong hand-shake.

The crew now consists of a super butch, a snoring girl, a wacked-out sicko pervert, a roaring tiger, and his intense, workaholic brother. We're missing the homophobic nun to wipe the smile off the dyke, a coffee distributor guy to wake up the snoozer, and a priest to "cure" the perv.

A shipment of trees, plants, and flowers was delivered yesterday. Paco's weekend crew placed them according to the design. I look around me, and everything's a huge pile of trees, like a messy jungle.

Jaylene rubs the nubs on her head while everyone just stands around as if waiting for instructions. I know they know what to do; they're probably just testing me.

I remind them, "My uncle Paco wants us to push the plants back and dig the holes *exactly* where the plants were."

"*Bárbaro,* dude!" Che grabs a shovel and gets to digging right away. He's working right next to me, showing off his scrawny, popped-out muscles. It's weird to look at the girls on his arm. Every time a muscle moves, they squirm around. Maybe he gets more action from watching his arm than in real life. Who knows.

I start digging a hole that's three feet in diameter and in depth. Then I'll stick a small bottle palm in it, shovel the earth back into the hole, and plant a bed of purple flowers around it.

Che points to El Tigre. "That guy came alone from Cuba in a *balsa* in shark-infested waters in secret, without telling a soul. And that dumbo-eared fat girl with the guy's haircut"—he juts his nose in Jaylene's direction—"she's a *tortillera*. If you're not careful, she'll soon be after your tail."

Harsh school memories crowd my brain. My heart beats fast. The palms of my hands get sweaty, and I wipe them on my overalls. I stand on the shovel and jump on it a few times to loosen the earth under me. "She won't get *my* tail, that's for sure." I had to say *some*thing so he doesn't think I'm a weirdo lesbo homo, even if in my heart I'm saying, "So *what* if she is?"

He whispers so that Jaylene, who's across from us, doesn't hear. "Don't be fooled. Those girls will haunt you till they catch you. Just be careful." He sniffs the air. "I can smell them a mile away. They're good for nothing, and they prey on beautiful, straight girls like you."

"I can take care of myself," I assure him. "Ain't no girl coming near *me*." It feels good to be talking this way to a guy who doesn't know about me having been in a long-term relationship with a girl. But I hate the way he's talking about Jaylene.

"Girls should be feminine like you and Camila, not shave their heads to look like guys." He juts his chin toward Jaylene. "I can turn any *invertida* around." I don't say a word, but he goes on. "Once *tortilleras* have a taste of me, they *never* go back." He raises his voice. "They just need a *real* man."

I feel like telling him he could stick his shovel where the sun doesn't shine, but I don't.

Jaylene overhears and comes over to us. She wraps her stubby hands around the shovel handle.

"A *real* man?" She bores holes into his pupils. I love the way she stands up to him.

He spits on the ground. "Yeah, want to try me?"

"I'm a hard-core bisexual, up with the queer movement, not insane. Your type just doesn't do it for me, crud bud." She says it loud enough so everyone hears. Everybody looks up and stops working. My stomach jumps inside me. I've never heard anyone talk that way about themselves in public, especially not in a group of straight Cubans. She's probably courageous because she's a gringa.

"Hey guys, Chago's coming back soon," I tell the crew, and surprisingly they get back to digging. All I need is another gay hell following me everywhere I go. I keep digging, trying to mind my own business; but Jaylene stays put.

"You know what they say, don't you?" Jaylene asks Che. He shrugs his shoulders. "Well, I won't give you the pleasure of finding out." She leans over and whispers in my ear. "They say imbecilic macho ignoramuses like him have small, shriveled-up worms. They have to prove their masculinity by talking shit. You think any bi or lesbian would ever go for *him*?" She swings her head back and blasts out a ratlike shriek.

I want to crack up and fall over laughing, but I don't. I swallow the laughter. I don't need anyone hating me on this job. I just have to play it wise.

Jaylene is the first to finish the biggest hole of all. Without asking for help, she picks up a small but heavy date palm tree and places it in the hole she dug. She throws in the rest of the soil and pats down the earth. She plants white, lancelike flowers in a circle around the tree and goes for the hose. She knows her stuff.

Che is having a hard time with some coral rock. He's hitting the rocks extremely hard with the shovel, with a lot of force, trying to break them loose. "*Oye.*" He looks up at me as he wipes sweat off his brow. "She's just acting tough to get my attention. I bet if I asked her to my pad tonight, she'd come."

That's all Jaylene needs, a worm after her butt.

"Ask her and see." I stick the shovel in a crack on the earth and whack my foot hard against it, imagining that it's Che. I'm cracking open his skull to plant colorful flowers in there. He needs something pretty to shake up his messed-up head.

"Those bis will screw anybody. I better stay away from her if I don't want AIDS."

He continues to shovel.

Time passes quickly, and before you know it, Tazer gets home. Chago comes back and deposits the trees and the mulch. He picks up Jaylene and they're off to the warehouse nursery. Tazer comes by with *croquetas de pollo* and cold pineapple juice for everybody.

"*¡Gracias!*" The crew throws down their shovels and runs to the snacks.

Tazer and I walk away from them and stand under a tall, bushy, gumbo-limbo tree. He's looking really handsome in khaki pants and sandals and a dark, forest green tank top that shows long, lean muscles.

"*Oye, chica,* you look sweeeeeet." He smacks me a kiss on my cheek. "You okay?"

"I'm great. Hey, thanks for dropping me home last night. Sorry I was so wacked out about the Betrayer." I stick my hand in my overalls pocket and bring out a smooth turquoise-colored stone I took from my rock collection. It's got a thin black streak around it. "For you." I love to give natural things such as rocks, leaves, and hand-picked flowers I've dried to people I really like. Gifts like that mean something special, and you can save them forever.

He scrutinizes it as he rubs his fingers over its smooth surface. "It's so cool. I love it. Thanks."

His thick, dark eyebrows and sparkling hazel eyes are amazing to look at. His skin is as smooth as a mango peel. It's too bad Tazer dyes his hair with chemicals. Maybe I can get him to change his mind about going back to his natural hair color.

"You look stunning in boots." His smile radiates.

"Right!" I roll my eyes. "And you look femmy in pants."

"Not!" He lets out a smooth laugh.

"Hey, where's your dad?" Chago needed to show him the backyard design I drew with Paco's help last week, when I didn't realize we were going to Tazer's house. Paco pointed to the trees and plants in a book, and I drew them. It was a piece of guava.

"My dad, well . . . like I told you at the beach, he's hardly ever around." He stares at his long fingers. "I practically live alone with our maid, Sulima. My dad works all the time. He's a great guy but he's only here when he's got an appointment."

Tazer's really spilling it out. I like that. I'm glad he feels comfortable telling me such intimate things. I guess he can see I'm a pretty trustworthy person.

"Now that he's rich, he flies all over the place on business trips every weekend. If I didn't have a picture of him, I might not know what he looks like."

His words remain floating in midair. He tries to smile, but I can see right through him. I totally get it. I haven't seen Mami in a while now, and it hurts. And Papi, well . . . he was the greatest dad who ever lived. He read me comics when I was sick and took good care of me. He loved me more than life itself. But now he's gone, and all I have is pictures and memories.

We move farther away from the crew and stand under another gumbo-limbo tree full of oval, dark green leaves.

"That sucks. Do you ever miss not having a mom?" I lean my back against the cool-feeling copper-red bark, stuff the *croquetica* in my mouth, and wash it down with a sip of delicious pineapple juice.

"Not really. At this point, I don't miss what I don't know and have never had. But I still miss my family in Cuba." His smile reassures me. "What's great is that I have no one on my back telling me what to do." He changes the topic. "How are you feeling about your ex?"

He wants to get to the core of *me*. The more we talk, the more I like him. He's smart, rugged, yet tender all at once. He's got a softness about him and a strong, sensual voice that matches his slender, muscular boi body. And he's generous, and sensitive, in a sweet boyish way. I can tell he's a fun, deep, smart, and good person with a great heart.

I cover the glare of the sun leaking through the branches with the palm of my hand. "Better, thanks," I lie.

"I didn't tell you yesterday, but hell, do I know what being dumped is like. I know what you're going through, Laura. My ex-girlfriend, Dori, broke it off last year after two years, out of nowhere. That night I went to her place, and there she was with a football player guy." He scrapes pieces of peeling bark from the tree with the stone I gave him. "The big, husky guy came to the front door and shook my hand when she introduced me as her cousin."

"Her cousin?"

"Yeah. She told everyone we were cousins. I could only go over when her parents were on vacation. We spent a lot of time here, but we couldn't be together at all in public because I look like a guy." He makes a weird face. "Homophobic

145

Miami." He goes on. "Being a boi is what Dori loved about me. She wasn't like the typical femme who wanted me to identify as a butch. I still miss the way she accepted me as a boi, even if like every closeted girl in Miami, she wouldn't be seen with me in public."

"That sucks." I know what he means about girls not wanting to be around him in public. I'd be terrified to chill with him in straight places, too, where everyone can point fingers at us and whisper to one another about what disgusting people we are. It's okay here. The crew sees Tazer as the dyke daughter of the guy who hired us. And it would be fine in gay places, too. But definitely not out in Miami. He really does look like a hot, sexy guy.

I don't know what to say, so I keep my trap zipped.

Tazer gets the message and puts a hand on my shoulder. "I guess you too would be scared to be seen with me in public, huh? You wouldn't be caught dead with me at the corner store, right?"

I'm caught off guard. "Well . . . uhh . . .

well . . . Let me put it to you this way. . . ." I jump in and tell him about Marlena's love letter—but I don't say her name—and the way I was treated afterward and how Mami threw me out of the house. It just pours out of me. But I lie like a fiend. "She was this really butch bull-dyke who was madly in love with me. I never liked her as more than just a friend. We never did anything, but she wrote in explicit detail about wanting to hook up with me." I go on and on.

His eyes widen. "Hell. The nun read it to the class?"

"Yup. It sucked." I look away from him, then smack into his eyes. "That dyke didn't look like a cute boi, like you. She looked like a sweaty wrestler lesbian. She had hairy legs, hairy pits, and she even had a bit of a mustache." I want to make the girl seem like the most macho dyke in the universe. "After all I went through because of that, no way will I even walk the streets with any-one who looks gay. It's too painful to be treated so horrible for nothing."

I had to make up this lie so he understands

why I won't be able to kick it with him in public places. I don't want to hurt his feelings, so fibbing is the only way out right now. When I get to know him better, I'll tell him the truth.

He lifts his arms. "I've got hairy pits." He points to his legs. "Check out the fuzz."

I feel my cheeks burn and don't know how to respond.

He dives in. "Relax. I know what you mean. In Miami, that's normal for a guy, not for a girl." He totally gets it. "Shit, I wish you had told me the day we met at the beach that your mom had just kicked you out. I would have understood, you know?" He looks at me with a sparkly puppy dog face, the type Chispita puts on when I pet her belly.

I look down at my working boots. "I know."

He bites the skin of his thumb. "Don't worry. I get why you didn't open up to me." His smile broadens as if he's seeing something glorious in front of his eyes. "But now that we're getting to be friends, I'm glad you're being honest and sharing with me."

Yeah, I'm more honest than a sinner in a confessional.

This sucks. What the heck am I doing? Here I am with a fantastic boi whom I could talk to truthfully about my life, and what do I do? I tell him lies. I'm getting smarter by the minute!

He scratches his square chin. "We don't have to go out into the straight world together. I'll order Italian and Cuban movies from Netflix. We'll watch them in my theater. We can be friends without anyone seeing us together. No problem. I'm used to it."

I don't have to explain. He knows ex*act*ly what's going on. To think that he understands and would be friends with me in secret, after everything I told him and all I've been through, gives me a loving feeling in my heart. If he's all for hiding, maybe eventually I can fall for him, even if I'm not attracted to him. Marlena was my type, and look what *she* did. I'll tell Tazer the truth about Marlena when we get closer and make him promise not to tell a soul. Things are looking up!

"That'll be great." I smile and look away from him.

A soft breeze comes our way, and he pushes his long bangs away from his face. We stand, just feeling the gust on our faces.

"Breezes like these make me believe there's a God. This is heaven on Earth."

It's true what he says. On such a hot, muggy day, this breeze makes me feel like we're floating on an ocean wave.

I sip the sweet drink, and it goes down as soft as rainfall. "You don't believe in a God?" I don't know exactly what he meant, and I want to make sure.

He crosses his beautiful arms over his flat chest and leans his broad shoulders on the tree. "I believe I'm one with everything and everyone who exists and existed, and together we make God."

I know lots of people who believe the same thing, but that's not my bag.

"That's cool, but I can't be part of things that are evil. No way could I be one with Hitler,

150

murderers, rapists, and crap like that."

"So, what do *you* believe in?"

"I believe in myself and in something I call Sacred Nature. Feeling one with nature soothes me. Nature feeds all of me. That's why I've gotta take care of her and keep her sacred. When I'm in nature, I feel like I belong. It's like I know where I come from and where I'm going."

"Nice." He cracks a big, juicy smile.

"I also believe in my little bro's love, and in my dog. They'd never hurt me or anyone else."

It's sad, but I don't think I'll ever trust anyone again but Pedri and Chispi. I no longer believe in people. They can turn on you in one second. And nature . . . well, it's always had its natural catastrophes before people polluted the earth, but now it's letting us know it's suffering greatly by expressing its pain with more severe hurricanes, earthquakes, and tornadoes. It's trying to save itself from the extreme pollution people keep making. I guess the way I see it is like this: If you're allergic to smoke and someone locks you in a room full of cigarette, cigar, and pipe smoke, you'd whirl around the room like a crazy maniac, too, trying to find a window to zoom out of.

I change the subject. "You don't use pesticides here, right?"

"Nope, why?"

I open up to him a little. "My dad died of kidney disease caused by pesticide poisoning. He was a horse groom, and he used to spray the horse corrals with that stupid crap to keep bugs away. The doc said pesticides seeped into his bloodstream and fried his kidneys." In Cuba, Papi was an engineer and a pilot, but since he didn't know a word of English, he ended up cleaning horseshit.

"That's awful. I'm sorry."

I lower my head. "Yeah. Thanks. I was thinking . . . You've got so much land, that after the landscape's installed, maybe I can come over and we can plant an organic veggie garden together. Then we can watch foreign films." I can't believe these words just slipped out of my mouth so easily. Little ole me asking a boi to get together! I wonder what I'll do next? Kiss him in public?

"Fo sho!" He goofs around and gives me a knuckle-to-knuckle punch.

I notice Chago parking and Jaylene climbing out of the truck and heading off to work.

"Hey, it was fun talking with you, but I've gotta go," I tell Tazer. "You got a boom box?"

He raises his voice to the crew. "Boom box time! Get ready for music!" He runs off and comes back with a huge ghetto blaster and puts on some blazing spit.

"*¡Música!*" the crew trumpets.

Jaylene makes up some cha-cha-cha steps on the spot and wiggles her fluffy bootie outta control. She looks adorable. "Cuban power!" She twirls once, twice—*uno, dos, tres*—then goes back to digging.

"Jaylene's definitely a butch dyke," Tazer assures me.

"Today she came out and told us she's bi. She calls herself *queer*."

"She's too butch to be my type. I like feminine girls. But you already know that, don't you?"

I look away from him and feel my cheeks

turning hot. I don't know if he's making a move on me or not.

I look around me. The rows of palms we've planted remind me of the Cuban countryside, of women on stilts with windblown hair. Soon the emptiness in Tazer's land will be transformed into a paradise. Maybe that will happen to me, too. While I work, I'll scoop out every bit of love I had for Marlena and plant a Tazer seed in my heart. Who knows? Maybe it'll grow into a beautiful tree. I don't know. Just maybe.

Act Natural!

I dash inside, pet Chispita vigorously, and give her tons of smooches. "Skooti-booti, I've missed you *so* much!" She slobbers all over my face. Her tail swings as fast as a windshield wiper, making her whole bootie twist from side to side.

Viva runs behind me with a mop in hand. "*¡Dios mío! ¡Ave María!* Take off those muddy shoes!" I hand them to her and walk around in socks. "I is gonna give Chispita a bath. Then," she insists, "I will boil your shoes."

I walk into the bathroom, peel off my muddy clothes, throw them on the floor, and jump in the shower. "Okay!" I yell to Viva. "Boil my shoes, add ketchup to 'em, and we'll have 'em for dinner. What the heck, we only live once!"

She lets out a sweet, musical laugh.

"Soli no cook today. She go to a boy's crib after work," she says from outside the bathroom door.

"Crib?" I laugh hysterically. She picked up our lingo!

She goes on. "All Soli Luna thinks about is boys, boys, boys!"

If Viva *really* knew the truth about Soli's crushes on guys and how she's dated all of Miami, she'd have a coronary and croak!

"Don't worry! I'll cook!" I boom from a stream of water pouring over me.

Viva is the only Cuban mother on this planet who doesn't even know how to boil milk. She burns toast and even adds salt when what is needed is sugar. She's a total wacked-out, differently-abled "chef."

I bathe and dress in tight button-down hip-hugger jeans, a thick brown belt, and a short, silky chartreuse Brazilian top that Viva ironed and hung for me on the towel rack. After getting so muddy and cruddy at work, I love to scrub till I'm squeaky clean, then dress nice, even if I'm just staying home. I've told Viva a million times not to iron my clothes, though. I hate it! But she doesn't give three cracked coconuts.

Viva's by her seven-foot statue of La Virgencita María, lighting candles and praying, as I sauté onions and green peppers in olive oil. When they get soft, I add sliced carrots, cubed potatoes, salt, oregano, and cumin. I stir-fry everything for ten minutes, then pour in one can of organic garbanzo beans and one of tomato paste. I throw in a few cloves of crushed garlic and a handful of olives and raisins. I cover the pot with a tight lid to cook while the white rice boils.

I learned to cook from helping Mami. I guess I just picked it up; it comes easy to me and I *love* it.

"*Boong-caboong-boong-bang!*" Soli's pounding on the front door gives us a jolt.

"Use your keys, nut case! We're not gonna open the door!"

Chispi flies to the door and slides smack into it. Soli leaps into the living room like a wild panther in heat, smelling slightly of perfume. "Yuk!" I hold my nose. "You're a friggin' stink bomb!" I go around opening the windows. Then I make her wash behind her neck and ears.

"Mima, Looly, I'm in *love*, totally *enamorada*!" Soli dances around doing the sixties' Funky Chicken in the skintight orange miniskirt that she's wearing under a guy's flapping white shirt. My little bean sprout howls and hops around like a bunny rabbit, wild with happiness. "I've fallen in love with Diego, Chispita!" She lifts the goopiwoopi's two front legs and twirls her around. Soli goes a little nutty once a month around the time of her period, so I don't pay her any mind. It's called PM Double S: Psycho Maniac Soli Syndrome.

I dice a tomato and throw it over the food, squeeze a lemon over everything, then pour a teaspoon of the juice the green olives are packed in and stir. "Right, Hootchi Momma. You're in love, ice no longer melts, and your bootie's gone flat!"

I serve the three of us. Viva brings three glasses of *jugo de melocotón* and a sliced avocado-and-onion salad to the table. She and I sit to eat.

Soli sticks her plate in the fridge. "I'm going out to dinner. I'll save it for later."

"Soli, you no cook or eat with us no more. Please, Soli Luna, sit and eat with us, like a family."

"Listen to your mom, creep head. She just came home from cleaning *four* houses." Viva hardly ever scolds her. She pretty much has no control over Soli, but she tries. "When your mom talks to you, it's like she's talking to a Cheez Doodle. You don't give a flying banana."

Soli picks at some garbanzo beans from the pan, sticks them in her mouth, and licks her fingers clean. "Mmmm . . . I don't have time to cook, Mima. Looly cooks delicious."

She washes her hands in the sink and wipes them dry on her miniskirt.

"Laurita work too. She clean up, organize, cook, and she help me with everyting."

I shoot Soli a steely look that means, *You could* at least *fake your mom out*. Soli always knows what I'm thinking and vice versa. No need to talk.

She kisses Viva's cheek. "Okay, okay, Mima. Chill. I promise to cook more often." She winks at me from behind Viva. I throw her a smile as I stuff my face.

"Bro, I'm serious," she goes on, all bright eyed. "I'm really in love with Diego."

I take a few tablespoonfuls of rice, throw them in the pan, and stir the rice around in order to suck up almost every drop of *salsita*. I pile the rice back on my plate and gobble up some more. "Right, and I'm a celibate priest wearing a bikini in outer space visiting alien sex fiends."

Soli cracks up.

Viva noisily scrapes sticky sauce from the pan and shoves a spoonful into her mouth.

"*¡Qué rrrico*, Laurita!"

I love when people like my food. It makes me feel like they love me tons.

Soli opens the fridge and finds a leftover chicken drumstick from Pollo Tropical.

"Yo, organic celibate nun, I redid Tazer's

bangs in blue, blond, black, and red streaks, just a few minutes ago."

"Why not give him ammonia to drink? That might make his skin grow vivid patches and leak in bright colors to match his gorgeous hair."

Soli laughs her ass off. She tackles the tough chicken fat between her front teeth and pulls at it with her thumb and index finger. "Tazer was my last appointment. He's so incredible. We're meeting at Cha-Cha's at seven thirty tonight; it's a gay Cuban organic veggie restaurant that just opened. Can you be*lieve* it?" She throws the drumstick back into the fridge and takes the fork from my hand. "Stop gorging! You're coming with us."

"I'm not going out to dinner, dingbat." I grab my fork. "Can't you see I'm eating with your mom?" I try not to act excited about my friendship with Tazer. Soli will stuff him down my throat till I'm nauseous. If anything's going to happen with Tazer, I want it to happen naturally, without Soli getting involved and spoiling everything. "And besides, I already saw Tazer today."

"Well, at least come greet Diego. He thinks

you're amazing, Looly. He wants to say hi. He's out in the car. Come on!"

"Snap, Soli, you've got Diego waiting out there all this time? You're so rude." I hope one day she finds someone who won't put up with her crap. That'll be the day she might fall in love.

"I no teach you bad manners, Soli Luna. Tell Diegito to come eats with us. We got *mucho* food to share."

A flow of merengue music rides the wind into the duplex from Soli's car. We stay quiet, listening to the jammin' beat that moves me to go outside and chill with Diego. He's damn blazin'. I like him better than any of Soli's other boy toys.

I stick my plate in the fridge and kiss Viva's cheek. "You won't get mad, will you?"

"No, *mijita*. You go and has some fun." I follow Soli outside. Viva holds on to Chispita so she doesn't chase us.

I run out with arms spread wide. "Diego!"

He climbs out of the car. We hug and kiss each other's cheeks.

"You's looking *fly*, little bird. Wazzz hangin'?"

His silver grill makes his top and bottom teeth shine. He's got silver chains hanging from his neck with medals of saints encrusted with diamonds. Diego's a hunk and a half.

"Just chillin'." I smile.

He rakes back his spiky, pitch-black hair. "Come kick it wit us." He's wearing a tight black T-shirt that shows a six-pack and supermuscular shoulders and arms. His very loose-fitting jeans are practically falling off him, showing his underwear.

Before I can say a word, Soli insists with the speed of a reckless car, "Bro, you're coming *with* us, and that's *that*!" She pushes me into the car. "To Cha-Cha's!"

Soli drives like a friggin' maniac, zooming down the expressway, swerving from lane to lane as we pop around like popcorn in our seats.

She squeezes into a tiny parking space and darts out of the car. Diego, looking psyched, bolts after her. I spring out as if someone's put a torpedo up my butt. We dash down the Miami Beach boardwalk like rock stars followed by millions of roaring fans.

Everywhere we look we see people skating, bicycling, or just walking. There are lots of muscular, pretty gay boys in sleeveless white shirts, cut-off jeans, and working boots, and lots of butch girls, all walking and talking. The straight right-wing Cubans in suits look at them with disgusted faces.

A storm is creeping our way. I feel it coming. It's getting gusty. The clouds are changing from puffy whites to sheets of dark gray, and it starts to drizzle.

We hurry to avoid getting wet and wait under a tarp for the rain to stop. I see Tazer under a canvas umbrella watching a row of Afro-Cuban women dancers and drummers on a stage. He dashes to us when he spots me. He's wearing a green basketball shirt, almond-colored pants, and brown leather boots. He looks kind of like a handsome prince.

Tazer kisses my cheek, then Soli's. He and Diego shake hands.

"You look goiiigious, Laura." He sounds happy as a conga beat.

"You too, Tazeroni Macaroni." He looks as masculine as Diego.

Soli slaps him a low five. "Beauteous dye job."

"Yeah, this genius haircutter restreaked it for me today. I wanted more colors. She's astounding." They laugh as Tazer adjusts his small, square, purple sunglasses. The rain has stopped but the night is windy, and our hair is flying all over the place. The ocean waves are crashing against the boardwalk, and we're getting sprayed. It's a perfectly romantic night, and if I can jumpstart my heart for Tazer, everything will be all right, outta sight, blue and white!

With a mighty swing of her hand, Soli insists "Let's go!"

We sit at a small table in a cozy corner of Cha-Cha's under a humongous, luminous umbrella near the crashing waves. It's beautiful out here, but I miss Marlena. Why? Why must she still be stuck in my heart? I take a deep breath and exhale.

The conversation whirls around, from Tazer and me meeting at the beach, to me quitting school and working full-time, to Soli meeting Diego at Books & Books and the following day cutting his hair. Soli tells Tazer, "He's a motorcycle mechanic, not just a part-time DJ. Look at him." Her right eyebrow arches and her pupils dilate. "He's the most delicious guy in the world."

"Yah, dawgs. I'm ill. Sick. The most ri*dic*ulous pimpin' gangsta *ever*." He gives out a robust laugh. "I'm goddesses' gift to birds."

Soli's right. He's superhot. And besides, he's got a blazin' personality to die for.

She kisses him and takes a bite out of his cushiony lips. "We took one look at each other, and it was love at first bite. I'm gonna marry him." Soli's stomach rumbles, and Tazer lets out a rugged laugh. What Tazer doesn't realize is that Soli's stomach can't go long without a guy. She's starving for Diego, practically doubled over with hunger, dying to eat him up like Kentucky fried chicken, finger-lickin' good and all that other crap.

Everyone's talking a mile a minute about this and that when our waitress walks to our table. Our eyes meet, and I lower mine to the floor. My heart is doing a strange thing inside my chest, like a rumba.

"Hey guys, I'm Gisela." She leans forward, and her loose, silky, leafy green blouse dances around her dark, clove-colored skin. "All meals come with wild rice or whole wheat Cuban bread. What'll you be having today?"

I want to say, "You, please," but I can't get the words out of me. My hands are trembling something fierce. I bet she's noticing. How embarrassing.

Soli points to number 9 on the menu. "I'll take the Homo Hummus with lots of Cuban bread and a Messy Mango shake." She slides her finger up to number 1. "He'll have the Faggy Frijoles with rice and a Big Banana shake." Soli takes control. Diego's *defi*nitely not a *machazo*. "For dessert I'll have the Tortillera Turrones, and he'll have the Dripping Dyko Donuts."

Tazer hands Gisela the menu. "Number 13. The Lesbo Lentils with rice and a side each of

Pounding Plantains and Tranny Tamales. To drink I'd like a *mandarina* fizz and for dessert the Genderqueer Gelatin."

I stare at my menu and don't dare look up into Gisela's large, sparkling, droopy eyes, which are lingering on mine. "Number 7. The Flaming Fembo Frijoles with *mariquitas* and a small Prissy Sissy *mamey* shake, please." I look up into her dark eyes. "Thank you." She's so yummy. Just having her near is making me hungry.

Gisela tosses her unruly, curly-wild, mahogany mane to one side and scrutinizes me in one long swoop. "The Fembos are my fave, too." My eyes dart fast around the restaurant and land on hers. I smile, cross my hands over my chest, uncross them, and cross them again. I am such a dingbat!

Tazer asks her, "What's going on around here? Why all the balloons and banners?"

Gisela smiles, and her pudgy nose scrunches up. "A lesbian film producer celebrated the opening of her movie here last night. Afterward, a group of us went next door to catch the documentary—it's based on Miami Beach's gay community. I love being part of the beach's *tortillera* scene."

I can't believe she used that word to mean something great.

Gisela looks like a disheveled poet, like she just bolted out of bed, showered, slipped on the first thing she found, and didn't fuss about her looks. Everything about her seems to gleam, including her two slightly crooked front teeth and clear braces.

Someone from another table calls her. Gisela winks at us. "I'll be right back with your food." She bolts and leaves the sweet scent of apple pie floating around us. I want to sniff the air and keep her scent inside me, but Soli will make a huge fuss over it.

A velvety cloud dances in my brain; I close my eyes and let this feeling flow.

"Way to go!" Soli whispers loudly, and I'm slapped out of my dream state.

"I think Gisela's into you," Tazer follows in a deep whisper, right in my ear.

Diego's eyes widen. "Yah, little bird. She be hot for ya."

"Cut it out, guys. She's gonna hear you. And besides, I'm not gay." I gently kick Soli's shin under the table.

I'd be so embarrassed if Gisela heard them going on like this; but in all honesty, I'm psyched they think she likes me. This is the first time since Marlena that I'm into a girl who might be attracted to me. But how could I possibly let her know I'm into her, too? I don't know how gay girls do it. I just know that it came easily for Marlena and me.

Tazer gently punches my arm. "You're too feminine for her. She needs a boi like me." He makes a muscle that pops out of his arm. "I've been working hard at the gym. Like it?"

Before I can answer, Soli leans over and grabs it. "*Huyyy*, almost bigger than Diego's."

Tazer cracks his knuckles. "Gisela looks a bit like my friend Clarissa, except Clarissa is thin and has short hair." His eyes brighten. "I've been heavy into drama and scriptwriting at school.

Clarissa wants to be a novelist. We just finished a play."

We're all ears.

"Check it out. The best scene goes like this: The mom of the girl in our lesbian script finds her in bed with another girl. Right before her mom faints, the girl screams to her lover, 'Act natural! Act natural!'"

Everyone lets out a hearty laugh.

Soli slaps Tazer's shoulder. "You're such a homo." She twirls a few dreadlocks around her index finger. "I'm surrounded by homos. What's this world coming to?"

She points a finger at me. I step on her foot hard under the table. I don't want her to out me to Tazer. I've lied to him, and he won't like it one bit. "This one's a homo. . . ."

"Sapien!" I shout, and the girls at the next table look over at us. The hum of the soft background music becomes a roar. I clear my throat and smile as I shred my napkin into pieces, then roll the pieces into a ball. Soli gets the message and shuts her trap. I'm a bigger dork than I originally thought.

Suddenly I have an urge to tell Tazer the whole truth when we're alone. The lying is getting to me.

Gisela places our food on the table without taking her expressive eyes off me. It feels as if she's wrapping her warmth around me. "Enjoy." She smiles a smile of ice-cream cones with sprinkles as she walks to the next table.

¡Ay, ay, ay!

Soli, Tazer, and Diego yack up a storm about this and that. I look around me and see girls holding hands with their lovers as natural as if they were drinking a glass of water.

I just don't get it. Aren't these people scared of their parents finding out?

I wish I could go up to Gisela and strike up a conversation. I'd ask her to come with me on a long bike ride along the beach, then a picnic in the moonlight. I want to kiss her so badly it hurts!

While Soli and Diego take a break to kiss, Tazer whispers to me, "I'm jealous. Gisela definitely likes you. Here I am thinking I'd be *her* type, and she ends up going for *you*."

"Just cuz she looks feminine doesn't mean she has to like the opposite of her or that she'll act like a wimpy fembo in bed." This slips out of me.

"And how do *you* know that?" Tazer squints.

"I've heard about it. I bet some butches and bois like you are softies in bed and some girls who look feminine like me are crazy-wild."

He lets out a suave laugh. "You're right. My ex looked feminine and took total control in bed. I loved that about her."

I quickly change the subject. "If you're into Gisela, go for her."

"She's not my type with that frizzy hair and solar-energy, intellectual look. Don't get me wrong. I can get into big, curvy girls with junk in their trunk, but I'm just not into the environmentalist-looking types. The braces don't do it for me either. You're all natural, but you don't look it or flaunt it. Know what I mean?"

"Yeah." I feel relieved that Tazer isn't into her and change the topic. Now *I* start yacking with everyone about this and that.

We finish our meal. On our way out I sneak a card with the name, phone number, and address of the restaurant into my pocket.

Hatin'

I park my red, tall-handlebar bike, which I painted with yellow-orange flames, in Tazer's shed. I'm glad Paco isn't around. Since today's our last day working here, Tazer invited us for breakfast at 6 A.M. Chago won't be here till seven o'clock.

"Hey! *¿Qué pasa?*" Tazer kisses my cheeks. "Those are mighty fine-looking golfing slacks." I smile. I love wearing my jade green, checkered thrift-shop pants.

"You're looking mighty blazin' yourself." He's wearing blue jeans and a maroon T-shirt with large yellow letters that say I Don't Bite. Tazer is gorgeous to look at, but I wish he looked more like Gisela.

I kiss his cheek and sing, "Tazeroni Macaroni was riding on a pony, eatin' some baloney. . . ." He cracks up. "Hey, I can't wait to chow down. I'm starved." He's looking at me with love in his eyes, and I can't stop thinking about Gisela. How messed up is *that*? But I'm such a chicken. I'll probably never call Gisela *or* date Tazer.

Camila's big brother drops her off, and he waves good-bye. We greet each other with kisses on our cheeks.

Che honks, shouts "Yo, Dudes!", and parks his dented pick-up truck in Tazer's driveway. Everyone except Jaylene is riding in the back. The rowdy crew piles out next to us.

"Where's Jaylene?" I ask.

Che bites off his gloves and stuffs them in his blue jean shorts pocket. "That stinking queer? You're out of your mind if you think I'd let her ride in *my* truck." Like his vehicle was his teeny ding-dong! I'd rather ride to work on a mule than in *his* stupid truck!

Tazer dives in. "Hey, it's not like she's going to rub her dykeness on your truck and leave a big queer smudge." I'm surprised Che hasn't talked bad about Tazer yet. It's probably because he's working for his father.

Out of nowhere Francisco, better known as Luscious Lesbo, drives in through the gates in a black Jeep. My jaw drops open. He gets out and introduces himself by shaking hands with everyone. "I'm Francisco. Just came to talk to Laura for a sec."

I look to Tazer, who seems as confused as me. What the heck could this guy be doing *here*?

He takes me to the side, away from everyone, and stops under a tall coconut palm tree. "Soli told me you were working at this address today." He goes into his pocket, pulls out a rubber band, and ties his long, wavy hair back into a ponytail.

I look up at him and sway from foot to foot. "So?" My heart is racing something fast.

I don't know why I'm giving Scum the time of day.

"Just wanted to tell you how sorry I am. I didn't

know Juan was spiking the drinks with Xs." His dark eyes meet mine, and they seem honest.

"That was pretty messed up." I take a few steps back. "What a jerk of a friend. It's kinda disgusting, really. Does he do that to *every* girl?" I've heard of guys drugging girls and driving them to their apartments, then taking advantage of them. Sicko pervs aren't my idea of fun.

He shrugs his shoulders, lowers his eyes, and stuffs his large, bony hands into his tight black jean pockets. "It was my birthday. I turned eighteen, and he gave me and all my friends free drinks." He stares at his red high-top sneakers. "I didn't know he was spiking the drinks with Xs. Trust me, Laura. You've got to believe me. He knows I'm not into drugs." He shakes his head. "I've already cussed him out. I'm really sorry."

"It sucked." I don't feel much like talking to a guy who has a friend who's a psycho perv.

"I know. But you've got to believe that I had nothing to do with it." He kicks a rock out of the way. "Soli told me you're seventeen. I thought you were my age. You look older."

"So what? Does that mean it's okay for that jerk to drug me without my knowledge?" I'm getting really pissed now.

"That's not what I meant. I told Juan he could be put in jail for drugging a minor. He's really crazy. I'm not talking to him again." He grabs my hand and blurts out, "I hope he didn't screw it up for me and you. Can we go out sometime?"

I'm taken aback. Suddenly, out of nowhere, this guy comes here to ask for my forgiveness *and* ask me out? That's too weird. What else can happen? Is Chispita going to start talking? Will Viva begin to bark and howl in the middle of the night?

I tell him the truth. "I'm going through a breakup right now. It's painful, and I'll probably be a terrible date."

He steps in closer to me and says with a twinkle in his eyes, "I don't mind being your rebound."

I get back to the old topic. "Why did you walk away at Papaya's and not confront Soli?" I thought he was a punk-ass chicken to do that. I wouldn't date such a wimp.

"You saw how Soli got. We work together, for crying out loud; but she hasn't even let me say a word to her till today. I thought I'd have a better chance of seeing you again if I left Soli alone so she could let off steam. I even had Juan call her and talk to her. He told her I knew nothing, that it was *his* fault."

"Oh." I don't know what to say. I guess he's being honest. If Soli talked to him, it must mean he's cool.

Just as I think I might muster up some courage to call Gisela or even give Tazer a chance, this happens. A *guy*, of all things, comes into my crazy life!

There's a weird silence between us, and he breaks the ice. "So, what's your sign? I'm an Aries. I bet we were meant to meet."

"I don't know a thing about astrology, but it seems to box and label everybody. I'm no robot." I won't give him an inch. "I don't act like my sign says I'm supposed to anyway."

"I'm not really into astrology either, but most

girls are, so I laid that one on you."

"Genius move, player." He chuckles. I look at my watch. "Hey, thanks for coming and explaining, but I've gotta get back to work."

"I've got Soli's number. She says you're living with her. Can I buzz you?"

I look away from him, toward the crew. "Yeah."

We kiss each other's cheeks good-bye and walk toward his car.

As Francisco is about to climb into his Jeep, Che grabs him by the arm. He slaps his back. "Dude, you're a lucky dog. You've got the prettiest girl in Miami."

Francisco shoves his hands into his jean pockets. "Me?" I look up at a cloud and watch the sun slide out from behind it. A good omen.

Che winks at me. "My friend Pincho El Flaco was at Papaya's on Sunday." His friend Pincho comes here on his lunch breaks. He and Che smoke weed and shoot the shit when Chago or Paco aren't around. "Pincho goes to all those mixed clubs to try to pick up *tortilleras* for threesomes. I wouldn't be caught dead in one. He saw you kissing a tall, thin guy with long black hair." He slaps Francisco's shoulder. Must be you, no?"

Francisco lets out a sleek laugh. "I don't kiss and tell."

Jaylene drives in with her little blue truck. Saved by the *belle*! "Hey, guys!" She's always supercheery.

Tazer gives her a big, husky hug. They slap each other's backs like football players do. They're becoming close friends.

I kiss her cheek. "What up, Keen Mean Jaylene?" She giggles and kisses me back.

Francisco introduces himself, and they shake hands.

Jaylene greets everyone else. Che doesn't greet her back. I guess she doesn't care *what* he thinks of her.

George pats my back. "So, you and Francisco, eh? Nice couple."

"What's going on?" Jaylene asks.

Tazer shrugs his shoulders. "Your guess is better than mine."

"It's not what it seems." Francisco tries to explain.

Everyone teases him. "Yeah. Yeah. We know."

He stops brushing aside the comments. I think he's liking the idea, cuz he can't take the big grin off his face.

Everyone keeps teasing us, so I cave in with a triumphant smile. It feels great to be getting so much positive attention. I goof off. "A'ite. A'ite. So we kissed, okay? So what, dawgs?"

Francisco plunges in. "Yeah." He looks at me with gleaming eyes. I slowly look away.

El Tigre sings in Spanish, "Love is in the air!" He slaps Francisco on the back a few times.

I'm feeling pretty damned accepted. I hate to admit it, but the Betrayer was right. This beats being spit at in the face. It keeps a great big smile on my lips till I face Tazer. He stands with his hands in his pockets, staring down at his feet.

"Let's have breakfast. Follow me." Tazer waves his hand. "You too, Francisco."

Francisco grabs my hand, and I let him. "Show us around?" he asks Tazer. "I've never

183

been inside a mansion."

"All right. Let's go!"

We follow Tazer through the arched entrance of the coral rock mansion and walk around huge marble columns and through carved wooden doors.

The long, spacious hall opens into a living room with white marble floors that's as large as a skating rink. Light sneaks in through lavender windows. Tazer takes us down a long hallway with tons of mirrors, hanging chandeliers, and paintings, then upstairs. "It's got seven bed-rooms. This is the library."

I look around. The dark wood ceiling, gigantic windows, and floor-to-ceiling bookshelves filled with books make me feel as if I'm inside a cathe-dral bookstore.

Everyone gasps. "Amazing! Crazy! Outra-geous!"

It's weird to be standing here thinking that some people live in cardboard boxes under the expressway.

Tazer takes us back down to the dining room.

The central air's temperature is freezing cold. Sulima grabs everyone's backpacks and places them on the sparkling floor next to an elegant living-room couch of bone-colored velvet.

Crystal lamps hang by thin glass chains in different parts of the room and glow a soft, golden color. Bright flowers in glass vases are all around the dining room. The air smells like crushed gardenias. We sit at the table.

Our breakfast is plantain tortilla, *pastelitos de queso*, and *jugo de naranja*. Sulima—dressed in white from head to toe—brings in loaves of fresh, oven-baked Cuban bread that fill the dining room with smells of toasty butter.

There are tons of Cuban millionaires and even billionaires in Miami. I guess in some ways Tazer is lucky. But if I had so much money, I wouldn't spend it on a mansion for two. I'd build little domes for the homeless. I know Tazer feels the same way, but it's his dad's "castle," and there's nothing he can do about it.

We share a pitcher of *café con leche* with condensed milk.

"Breakfast for men!" Che trumpets. "And two gorgeous girls." He looks at Camila and me, lifts his orange juice glass, and cheers. He's such a psycho loser, this guy. I think men with little peepers have PMS, too: Peeper Mini Syndrome.

Francisco saves the day. He lifts his glass. "Here's a toast to Jaylene and Tazer." He lets out a sweet laugh. "I'm psyched that you four girls are here, because you guys are so ugly to look at." The guys laugh vigorously.

Tazer looks away. I can tell he doesn't like being seen as a girl. Regardless of his mistake, Francisco is sensitive and funny. I'm liking him a little more.

"Girls and guys should be treated equal," says George.

I lay it down like I see it. "True equality will happen when straight guys start dressing and acting like girls." I point to the guys. "Girls picked up all your bad habits—like drinking, smoking, hooking up with everybody, going to the gym to get muscles, wearing suits and ties to work—just to be equal. It's cool for butches, kings, and bois to dress like guys, cuz that's how they really feel. But for real equality you guys have got to start dressing in skirts and heels and putting on makeup."

I cause a real commotion. We all start serving ourselves the food and speaking politics in fast Spanish so El Tigre will understand. Luckily Jaylene speaks and understands Spanish from having taken Spanish courses in school. Her accent is cute, and kinda funny.

Camila delicately unfolds a napkin and places it on her lap. She sits quietly, while everyone else yapety-yaps.

Che launches a humongous piece of food into his Alaskan-sized mouth and changes the subject. He kisses his diamond-encrusted gold crucifix. "Thank you, God, for this food, for freedom, and for freedom of speech." He stuffs a stack of food into his mouth, gulps oceans of juice, and burps loudly.

Before I stick another forkful of food in my mouth, I close my eyes and make a wish to Sacred Nature. "I hope the millions of homeless in the world and the poor who can't buy food get to eat every day." I take a sip of juice.

Jaylene puts down her fork. "Yeah. And I pray for *real* freedom of speech. Gays, bis, trannies, and genderqueers here can't speak their minds."

With Francisco here and nobody knowing about my past, I feel courageous enough to express myself. "Yeah, here they have no rights. They don't have the same privileges as straights. Some even get killed."

Che lifts his cruddy index finger in the air. "Let them kill *all* fags!"

Francisco, Tazer, Jaylene, and I glare at him. George, Camila, and El Tigre remain silent. They seem scared to speak. I peer into Che's eyes. "Why do you hate gay guys so much? What have they done to you?"

He lets out a wicked laugh. "Okay, so *don't* kill them. Stick them all in jail so they can screw each other. AIDS cures faggots."

El Tigre excuses himself to use the bathroom. He looks flustered. Francisco keeps his cool. "You're cruel and ignorant, *mano*. A true compassionate hero." I like that Francisco speaks his mind, but I feel all riled up inside and I can't say a word.

Tazer wipes his mouth with a napkin. "What are you, in the antifag Ku Klux Klan movement? Are you an antigay Nazi?"

Jaylene grits her teeth. "He's just a disgusting, ignorant idiot."

Che's cheeks are a bloody red. He puts down his glass. "And what do *you* care about faggots? You're nothin' but a confused gringa bisexual." He tears a piece of bread in half, smears it with a truckful of butter, and takes a huge bite out of it.

I swig a sip of sweet *café con leche*, but it slides down bitter.

Tazer stands next to Che. "Leave my house."

Che stands up, and just as I think he's going to punch Tazer in the face, he grabs Tazer's hand and shakes it. "Sorry. I get carried away talking politics. I'm Republican and have strong opinions. That's what I love about America: freedom of speech. We're free to speak our minds." He knows Tazer's dad's got our paycheck. That's why he's shutting up.

El Tigre comes back looking refreshed, as if he's splashed cold water on his face. The tension eased and nobody became violent. Before you know it we're done with breakfast, and with the dessert—*casquitos de guayaba*.

Tazer smiles. "Let me show you guys something before you get back to slaving."

We follow him up the marble staircase that leads onto the third-floor terrace. You can see the waterfalls we made cascading into the pond we installed in the backyard. There's a stone path with swaying tropical fruit trees, coral rock gardens, a grotto, arches for climbing roses, and a pond with large koi, just as I'd sketched it for Paco.

"Wow! We did *that*?" Camila slaps her cheek, not believing her eyes.

We stare in silent awe at the beauty of what we built in one week.

I look at my watch. "Time to get back to work!" I clap my hands. "Last one down's a rotten mango!" In a fury, I'm running down the stairs and everyone's following.

We get downstairs, and I say my good-byes to Francisco. "I'm glad you came by." Now that I know he's honest about his apology, I like and respect him more.

He kisses my cheek. "I'll call you soon." I wave good-bye, and he takes off.

Tazer yells to me from his bedroom window, "Laura, come here a sec!"

I dash upstairs to the second floor and find Tazer leaning against the door of his bedroom with arms crossed over his chest. He walks into his empty room, which is being remodeled, and I follow. The chartreuse-colored walls reek of fresh paint. Intense music from my ancient, classic Doors CD leaks in from the boom box downstairs.

I stare out the window to see the crew taking shovels full of mulch and throwing them by the palm island. Jaylene is whistling up a storm.

"She met a really hot babe, Rosa, last night. Jay's in heaven."

I smile. "I can tell."

Tazer squints and puts on a grave expression. "Look, I know you got thrown out of Virgen María for being gay. You know how word spreads in Miami. I just never told you, so you wouldn't feel so bad about lying to me about 'Mario,' the Betrayer."

I feel heat climbing up from my heels to my head. Memories of the Incident fill my brain. I'm nervous that he'll tell Francisco and everyone here, and the good times the crew and I have had at work will end exactly as they did in high school.

Tazer doesn't take his eyes off mine. "So if you're gay and I totally get you, why can't you be honest with me? Are you turning straight now? If we're supposed to be friends, why do you keep lying to me like that?"

I swallow hard a bunch of times as I scan the empty walls. I tap my foot on the shiny wooden floor, and the sound echoes around the room. "I'm sorry I lied. It's just too hard to talk about this stuff." I can't believe the whole wacked-out world knows about me. Soon the crew and

Francisco will know, too.

"But I thought we were friends. Are you just pre*ten*ding to be my friend?" He seems upset, and I don't blame him. I hate being caught in a huge horrible lie. I've never lied like this before. And to someone so incredible and to whom I know I can talk to about Marlena.

"We *are* friends. I'm really sorry," I repeat. "I lied because of what happened to me. Please forgive me, Tazer, and don't tell the crew about Marlena and me. Lots of people hate me just cuz I was in love with a girl. And don't tell Jaylene, either. Please."

I explain in full, horrific detail everything I went through. I'm really terrified he's going to start spreading the word. Just when my life takes a great spin, something happens to mess it up good.

"It's too bad about what happened to you. If you don't want to tell Jaylene, that's fine with me. But you could've talked to me about what went down. I'm your friend, you know. I would've understood."

"It's just that I've never even *liked* any other girl but Marlena, until recently." I don't say it's Gisela. "I'm in a lot of pain. My mom doesn't love me just because I was in a relationship with a girl. If I want to live a great, happy life, I probably should never fall in love with a girl again, Tazer." I look into his eyes. "And besides, didn't you see what a commotion Francisco and I caused when they found out we had kissed? I like being treated with respect."

"Respect?" He juts his nose in the direction of the crew. "I hate to tell you, but I doubt that crew will respect you, except for Jaylene. None of them spoke up when Che said such an atrocity. They're probably all right-wingers. And Che is nuts. All that loathing. And he's wearing a crucifix. Jesus would die if he saw such shit. That's not what he was about." He peers into my eyes. "You're going to let *idiots* like those nuns, your ex-friends, and *him* rule your life?"

Tazer's so right. It's all about fear and ignorance. But it's so easy for him to say. He never had a neurohomophobic mom. And his dad doesn't give three royal monkey pubes about how he lives his life. He can come and go and do whatever he wants. Tazer's dad doesn't even know who Tazer's friends are. But I bet if he were a "normal" father, Tazer would be in my shoes. I've never heard of a Cuban right-winger dad accepting a gay child. The only Cuban parents on Earth who I think would accept gay children are people like Viva. She accepts everyone cuz she's full of love.

As if slapped in the face, I have a realization. I've never felt this strongly about anything. Francisco is my savior. Is it so wrong to want peace and acceptance from my mom and society and also want my family back?

I jam my hands into my pockets and kick away a bit of mud that fell off my boots. I cough and turn my eyes toward the crew. "I . . . I . . ."

Tazer interrupts. "Look. It's *your* life. You think you can fall in love with Francisco?"

I shrug my shoulders. "Maybe love grows." I remember Marlena's words about Ricardo, and I cringe. She did the same crap I'm doing now.

Tazer smiles a wicked, funny, twisted smile. "Well, in that case, if you can fall in love with *any*one, then include me." He reaches down and kisses my lips as Jim Morrison sings,

> *Tried to run; tried to hide.*
> *Break on through to the other*
>   *side.*
> *Break on through to the other*
>   *side.*

Up Yours!

I ride fast and furious to Pedri's school after work. He's behind the rest of his class in math and English and had to enroll in an after-school program. I reach the fence and park my bike. He runs to me.

"Laury!"

"Little Punk!" I swing him around. "You grew about ten feet since last week." I goof around and cover his little mushy face with kisses.

"Yeah!" He squishes his head against my stomach. "I'm big now."

In the distance, the roar of kids' happy screams fills the school yard.

I sit on the steps and put him on my lap. "I know Mami will be here to pick you up any minute, but I had to come to let you know something important."

"What?"

I kiss his sweet, freckly cheeks. "I'm going to work it out with Mami so she lets me move back home."

He leaps off me and jumps up and down. "Really?"

"Yup. But it might take a few months. You know how Mami is, and I have to do it slowly. Can you be patient and wait a long time, like half a year?"

"Yeah, Laury! I'll wait! I'll wait! But make it fast! Can't it be faster? Pleeeeeease?"

"I'll try, Little Punk. But no matter how long it takes, I'm almost sure I'm coming back home."

I find Viva outside. She's watering the organic tomato and cucumber seeds I planted for her, wearing a large, multicolored, two-piece bathing suit and a pink shower cap so her hair won't get fried. I notice a garlic clove stuck in her belly button.

I rush to her and pinch her butt. "Vivalini! Are you growing a garlic tree?"

"*Ay,* Laurita!" She lets out a silly laugh. "*Hola, mariposita.*" We hug and kiss each other's cheeks. "Garlics keeps evil espirits and *vampiros* away."

Chispita leaps all over me. I squeeze her in my arms. "Chooki-Wooki!" She licks and bites my nose with the sweetest baloney breath on Earth. I scrutinize her fur; it seems way lighter. "You dyed Chispita's hair?"

"No. No. I promise. She be out in the sun too much."

I see a bottle of hydrogen peroxide on top of the lounge chair and give a sigh of relief. I point to it. "What's that?"

"*Ay,* it's only nontoxic *peroxido.*" She crinkles up her nose and lets out a sneaky laugh. "I put a little in the floor of our crib because she pee inside. I use the rest to make Chispita a blondie."

"Chispita peed in our *crib*?" I want to die

laughing when she says *crib*, but instead I act upset and throw my hands up in the air. "Teaching you how to train a puppy is like teaching a noodle to run."

"*Ay*, Laurita, you is such a pain in the butt." She pinches my cheek, and we laugh.

I go inside and shower, then Soli helps me make *fricasé de* tofu with lots of organic veggies, stir-fried onions, and garlic. After dinner, Viva goes outside with Chispi to chill in the hammock and read astrology and saint magazines. Soli and I are hanging out on the living-room floor, facing each other, just chillin', listening to my primeval Phoebe Snow and Kenny Rankin vinyl records on Viva's archaic record player.

I bite off a piece of torn nail from my index finger and spit it on the ground. "You won't believe what happened. Francisco showed up at work today and Tazer—"

She smoothes down the hem of her neon purple spandex miniskirt and interrupts. "Looly, later on *that*. Man, I think I got an STD or herpes or something. I'm all swollen and stuff, and it itches and hurts like crazy."

"Jesus, Soli, you haven't been using condoms?" I can't even think about her being bed bound with AIDS and in extreme pain. It would be too much for Soli, Viva, *and* me to bear. Soli's in my heart. I love her like a sister, deep, deep down to the core. I don't want her to ever suffer.

"Bro! Of course I *always* use protection."

The dark circles under her eyes make her face seem droopy. I see her worried expression and hug her to me. "Don't fret, Hootchi Momma. I'll go with you to the gyno. It's nothing." I'm concerned and hope that the condoms she used didn't tear and that it isn't AIDS. You never know. It could only take one time to get it.

I talk to her for a while about what she's feeling and about Diego. I hate that she's so down in the dumps. She's madly in love with Diego and says, "I won't hook up with him again till I know what I've got. He couldn't have given me anything, and I don't want to give him anything either, in case it's from a past hookup." I've never seen her so down. What bad luck. I want to make sure she knows I'm here for her no matter what.

After I make her call the gyno for an appointment, she says, "I talked it out with Francisco at work. He's a good guy after all. I bet you freaked when he went to see you."

"Yeah. He totally flipped me out."

"He's so into you. Did you like making out with him at Papaya's?"

I throw off my sandals. "Well . . . it was . . . hard, different. He's got nubs. But he's so nice and sweet." Making out with a guy will never compare with kissing Marlena. Kissing Tazer was better than making out with Francisco, but I'm going to give Francisco a chance.

"Bro, when you talked about kissing Marlena, you were on fire. But: '*Nice* and *sweet*'? Nice is lying on the ground and kissing the grass. Sweet is kissing a ladybug. You need to kiss a girl again so you can see what you're missing."

I slap her cheeks as if they are bongo drums. "Well . . . in *that* case, Hootchi Momma . . . Tazer kissed me today. I know he's a boi, but he's still got breasts and everything else." I tell her the whoooooole story.

"Hallelujah!" She slaps me a high five and a low five, and sings out, "Looly got kissed by a genderqueer!"

I have to let her know the truth, even if she won't like it. "But I didn't get butterflies in my stomach. I didn't see shooting rockets, and planets didn't collide." It's true. Tazer is a fine kissing machine; he's got this smooth, wild tongue action. But the firecrackers just never went off. I let him kiss me, I really did. I stayed there and kissed him back till I could hardly breathe. And then I caught my breath, and we kissed some more. No one can tell me I didn't give Tazer a chance.

She shakes me by my shoulders. "Tazer is a guy, Looly. Kissing him is probably just like making out with Francisco. He's not your type. Now, if a girl you liked had kissed you, you'd have melted on the floor. I'd've had to scoop you up and bring you back to life!"

I laugh like a maniac. There's no hiding anything from Soli-Woli. She knows me better than anybody.

Beep, beep! Someone honks, and we rush to the door. It's Lazer Tazer, the fly kissing machine.

Soli zooms out through the back sliding glass doors. "I'll keep Mima company and leave you guys alone. Kiss him again and again! You might like it the one *hun*dredth time! Think of it as the first step to getting you onto the second step: kissing a lesbo!" She slams the back doors shut.

I let Tazer in. His smile glows. It fills the room with warmth. "You bailed so fast after work."

It's true. After we kissed and kissed, I got jittery and practically ran out, telling him I had to finish working. After work, I rushed out without even saying good-bye.

"I had to visit Pedri, then come home and cook."

We plunk down on the couch, facing each other. I notice that his chest isn't flat. He didn't bind his breasts, and he's got medium-small breasts like mine. They stand out because he's wearing an extremely tight white tank top T-shirt. He's letting his bangs grow longer, and he keeps tossing them away from his face.

I cross my left leg over my right and tap my thighs. I don't look at his face and don't know what to say, so I blurt, "Your hair's starting to look fly."

"Be careful," he jokes. "You might be falling in love with me." He uses his hand as if it were a mirror. He looks into it and fixes his hair with his free hand. "Being genderqueer doesn't mean I can't act fembo when someone I like prefers feminine-looking girls. Maybe if I stop binding now and then and grow my hair a little longer, you'd like me better, eh?"

I tap my foot on the floor: *tippy-tap, tippy-tip.* I uncross my leg and place my hands on my thighs. My eyes widen. "Hey!" I come up with the most wacked-out idea ever! "What if you turn me into a drag king and I make you up like a T-girl, just for fun?" This might keep his thoughts away from wanting to find ways to be with me. And it might also keep his twirling tongue action away from my mouth.

He sticks two of Viva's velvet cushions up his shirt; it makes his chest look as if he's got two big balloon boobs. "I want to be Booboola Anderson!"

I crack up. "Come on, Tazeroni Spazeroni! Let's change clothes." I goof around, and the tension flies out of me. "You can be Tazmina Mandarina, and I'll call myself Loreno."

Before he can say "I'm not wearing your miniskirt!" I've changed into his pants and T and he's got on my skirt and tiny stretch tank top. I've tucked my hair inside a baseball cap that I found in Soli's closet and stuck a banana inside my pants.

We look at ourselves in the mirror. He chuckles. "You'll never look like a boy, even while packing a big one."

I rush to Soli's all-natural, organic makeup bag, which I gave her for her birthday—before Tazer decides to start kissing me again—and come back with all sorts of eye makeup, blushes, and lipstick. I corner him against the end of the coffee table and powder his face with white powder. "I'm going to make you look like a geisha girl."

I want to see what Tazer would look like as a

Japanese girl. Not that I want him to change from a boi or that it'll change my mind about what I'm about to do with my life. And besides, I *hate* makeup.

Once his face and neck are ghostly white, I go to his eyes. I brush golden powder on his lids before outlining his eyes in black slants. "Wow, Tazer. You're starting to look like a *real* girl. Shit. Now you'll have butches after your butt!"

"Are you getting a hard-on?" He grabs my banana just for fun. I leap up, and we laugh hysterically.

I place fake eyelashes on him as he blinks up a storm. Then I paint his lips bright strawberry red.

I walk him to the nearest mirror. He flaps his eyelashes, grins, and turns to me. "Am I girl enough for you now?" He leans into me, grabs my face with both hands, kisses my lips, and goes into that wild tongue action motion that's smooth and soft but passionate. I love it. I love the way his slippery tongue feels in my mouth. But it's too weird to be kissing Tazer and focusing on his kissing style rather than feeling anything in my heart.

Soli walks in and surprises us. "Hell, yeah! You guys look amazing!" She sticks her hand into my pants, takes out the banana, peels it, and takes a bite out of it. "Tazer, man, you look like a real girl. That's wild." She turns to me. "You look cute, but still femmy. But hey, don't mind me. Keep struttin' your stuff. I'm outta here!" She makes a U-turn, but Tazer grabs her by the arm.

"Don't worry about it. I've gotta get going anyways. I should've already picked my dad up at the airport. He's going to throw a party when he sees my girly makeover."

He kisses my lips. "I'll call you tonight." Soli slaps him a high five, and Tazer rushes out the front door.

Soli gently smacks my face. "Man. He's a hunk as a guy, and a beautiful girl. Unbelievable. Was kissing Tazmina better than making out with Tazer? Huh, huh? Was it?"

"It was exactly the same. Tazmina is good, all right, but her kissing doesn't make me feel like crawling the walls." I wipe my mouth clean of lipstick with the back of my hand and slide the visor part of the cap toward the back of my head. "Crazy stuff, Hootchi Momma. You'd think I was bisexual at the rate *I'm* going." I would never in a million years have thought I'd kiss a guy, a boi, and then him as a girl all in the same week. I'm just not the type to be kissing around.

"But if he's good, will you give him a chance? I know he'll be into being a girl for you."

"Soli, man, he's not my type as a girl or boi. I love him as a friend, and I don't want to have sex if I'm not in love. He's sexual, like you, not romantic and sensual. He's not for making love with, got it?"

Tazer is the type who grabs you and kisses you and throws you on the bed. Feminine-looking gay girls can act assertive, too—that type of behavior doesn't need a butch girl or boi. But I like equal partnership, where nobody takes roles, and you and your partner are free to do what moves you. Tazer's aggressiveness toward me, though, whether as a boy or girl, lets me know he's totally into wanting me to be submissive. That just doesn't fly with me.

Soli squeezes my cheeks together, making my lips puff out like a fish. "Sissy stuff, that making-love stuff. You need a *real* lesbian, or someone like Tazer, Looly, to show you how gay you really are. With Tazer you've got it all: a boi who is still a girl underneath. You just have to keep giving him more chances. I bet he's superhot in bed."

Soli's starting to irk me. She won't leave it alone.

"I'm sorry to say I'm forgetting about girls or anyone who remotely resembles a girl underneath it all; it's just a big hassle that'll mess up my life even more. Tazer and Francisco both kiss about the same, but only one of them won't bring me any heartache. Can you imagine explaining to my mom that Tazer *is* a boy *and* a girl? She'll croak! It'll be a gazillion times worse than it was with Marlena. No thanks. I'm sticking with the one that'll free up my life of trouble."

Soli stares at me with her mouth wide open, as if I had chopped someone's head off. "You're *not* going to give Tazer a chance?"

"Nope. I'm going out with Francisco till I fall

in love with him. I need peace in my life. I've gotta get my family back."

"Christ, Looly." Soli sounds exasperated. "You know you're a big homo and you just need to find the right girl. I get it that Tazer doesn't do it for you. But there are a million gay girls who will. Going out with Francisco is stupid and a big, fat lie. You're doing a Marlena."

I *hate* what she just said.

I rummage around on the floor next to me for my small sketch pad. I find it under the TV and start sketching galloping horses without looking at her. I want her to go away. Just when I thought I'd made the best decision of my life, Soli comes and steps on it.

"Looly, man," she goes on, sitting down at my side, "just forget about Francisco. Go out with Tazer as just friends; you'll meet gay girls that way. He's probably got lots of lesbo friends. You're just traumatized cuz of what happened at school and cuz the Betrayer screwed you up."

I throw the sketch pad and pencil on the floor. "Didn't you hear what I just said about not wanting to go out with girls, bois, or anybody who looks gay? Nobody listens to me. When I told this to Tazer, he kissed me." I place the palm of my hand in front of her face. "Stop already! I swear, I'd rather get an enema from a gorilla than keep listening." I search the pile of CDs on the floor for some Reggaeton.

"Bro, you don't have to get so testy, OKAY?" She tugs at her nose ring and calmly lays her head on my thigh, hands clasped behind her head.

I scrub my face with my hands and set the CDs back down. "I just need to be left alone so I can figure out my life. I have to make my own decisions, all right?"

She stands and stares down at me with fists on her waist. "You've changed. You never lied to people, and now you're becoming the *biggest* liar. And you never used to get so pissed at me for any little thing."

I look up at her. "You're nuts."

She peels a piece of cracked orange polish off her fingernail. "You've never had such a strong personality." The peel drops on the tip of my big toe, and I leave it there. "You used to be the most fun girl alive. You're a different person since Marlena left you."

Her words insult me. In a heartbeat I spring up. We're *this* close, facing each other.

"Are you *toasted*? I'm *still* the same person."

"No you're not. You're no fun anymore, and you're going to go out with a guy when you know you're gay. Before Marlena, you dated Lorenzo and Manuel, and you didn't feel anything for them. You told me so yourself."

"I dated them when I was fourteen just because they asked me out. I didn't even *know* how to kiss. You know that the guy I really liked was Gustavo, but he wasn't into me."

"You wouldn't have felt anything for him, either."

There's a sad silence in the room. I don't want to have a fight, so I change the subject.

"I think you've got a mustard stain on your top."

"No, it's mango. Diego and I . . . er . . . well . . . forget it."

"What? Tell me."

"You don't care anyways." She walks to the living-room window. I jump over the piles of CDs, trying hard not to step on anything, and grab her arm.

"Jesus, Soli, I *do* care." I don't like it when Soli acts this way. She knows I love her.

She presses her forehead and nose up against the windowpane and fogs it all up. "You don't care what I think anymore. You don't listen to me, and you get pissed at me for everything. I don't need you anyways, Looly."

"You *do* need me, you turkey. Just chill on the gay thing, okay?"

I grab my Cuban architecture book from the floor, sit down, and leaf through it. She picks up one of my organic gardening mags, sits far away from me, and looks at the photos as if she were into it.

I put down the book. "Ever since my mom threw me out and Marlena split, I've had the worst times of my life. You and your mom are the only two people in the whole world who've been there for me." I scratch the tip of my nose. "You're the best friend anyone could ever have, so stop the crap and let me live my life like I want to live it. I don't tell you how to live *your* life."

She looks up from the mag. "Looly, you're my *best* friend. You *know* I'd chop off my dreads for you."

"I know. I know you'd rip out your eyeballs for me."

I smile, but she doesn't. Instead she says, "But it's stupid that you're gay and you're going to live a lie."

I wring my hands. I need to tell her what's in my heart. "Listen, Soli. I hate labels. If you want to label me, then I guess I was gay when Marlena and I were together. I was *totally* in love with her. I felt complete, and I never checked out another girl or guy. The truth is that I'm attracted to Francisco. It's not emotional, but everything else is there. This doesn't mean I'm bisexual. If I were to fall in love with him, I'd consider myself straight."

"Straight? You were deeply in love with a girl

for two and a half years, Looly!"

"I know! But I'm telling you the truth. That's the way it really is for me. The thing is that I don't know if I can fall in love with Francisco. If I do, I know I'll never look at another girl or guy in my entire life. That will mean I'm straight."

"Yeah. A straight who used to be gay." She gets sarcastic on me, but I don't pay her any mind.

"That's right. I need to go with my better judgment this time and not just with my heart and feelings. That got me into a lot of trouble. Get it?"

"Nope."

"Look. I also need my mom and Pedri in my life. I'll do anything to have them back. If being with a girl will keep me away from them, I'm going to go for a guy and try my hardest to fall for him. It still hurts so much. I'm so messed up, Soli. I just have to clear this mess of my life up for good, on my own."

She comes over to me, pulls me up by my hand, and wraps her arms around me in a hug. "Oh, I get it, Looly. It's about giving your mom, who threw you out of your crib, the satisfaction of seeing you with a guy." I loosen my hug and back away from her. "It's about lying to your mom so she can love you. Way to go, Looly! But don't say I didn't warn you."

I peel off the cap and throw it on the couch, and my hair comes tumbling down. "Didn't you hear or believe anything I said?"

"I heard you, but no way do I believe it."

"Screw you!" I belt out as I reach for the front door.

"Up yours!" she blasts as she slams the door behind me.

Get Me Out of Here!

My fight with Soli didn't last long. We were mad ten minutes. I walked around the block, and when I got back home we put on my Brazilian CDs and started dancing as if nothing had happened. We needed to wait a month for Soli's appointment at the community clinic, then another two weeks before the results. Luckily she only had a yeast infection that cleared before she saw the doc.

We've gone on with our lives and lots of great things have happened. Two months ago, in the beginning of July, Soli bought a two-seater minibike and we haven't stopped cruising Miami. Last month Viva got to meet Sai Mu. He came from India to give a spiritual workshop. And if that's not *fab*ulous news, listen to *this*: Paco promoted me to part-time landscape designer/sketcher and part-time tree installer. He gave me a big, fat, juicy raise! And I've been dating Francisco on weekends. I started seeing him the day after he visited me at work. We get along pretty well. I want to keep taking it slow, but he's driving me bananas about wanting to see me more often.

It's September 8, Astro Viva's fiftieth birthday. Early this morning Soli and I dropped off Viva and her best friend, Adela, at the Imax 3-D theater in Fort Lauderdale. It's La Caridad del Cobre Day, and traffic was the pits because of a procession carrying the Virgin statue along Calle Ocho. Afterward we headed to the dog pound, and I got Viva what she's always wanted: a bulldog mutt. Our neighbor is keeping the pup at her duplex till tomorrow morning for an even *bigger* surprise.

Diego comes by to help Soli and me clean,

organize, and prepare our place for the best party *ever*. We're working away when Tazer walks in. I open my eyes wide. He'd stopped talking to me cold the day I made him up as a geisha. I'd called him that night and told him I just wanted to be his friend and I was going to start dating Francisco. He'd said, "I'm not into being *just* friends." No matter how many times I called him or e-mailed him so we could talk things out, he wouldn't answer the phone or write back.

Tazer pulls me outside by the arm. We stand next to a pregnant banana tree. I'm really excited to see him and hope he doesn't chew me out.

He buttons up his fancy navy blue shirt, pulls on his purple suspenders, and sticks his hands in his navy blue pleated pants pockets. "Sorry I got so pissed when you said you were going to date Francisco." He looks away from me.

I grab a long banana leaf, pull it toward my nose, and sniff it. "It's okay. I'm sorry if I hurt you; I really didn't mean to." I have to make sure he knows I never wanted to play with his feelings.

"Yeah, I know. I got all your messages and e-

220

mails. I should've called you back, but I was hurt that you chose *him* over me." He stands on his tiptoes, squints, and checks out the scene indoors. "Is he here? Are you still dating him?"

"Yes, but I've broken up with him a bunch of times. He always talks me into getting back together. He's home with the flu, so he's not coming today." I peel a piece of the leaf and tear it into a few strips. I tell him everything that's been going on and the truth about why I'm trying to fall for Francisco and forget gay girls or bois. "Just too much for me to handle." If Tazer wants to be my friend, he's going to have to accept my life as I've chosen to live it.

"Are you still pissed at me? You think we can ever be friends again? I mean, *just* friends?" I really liked Tazer's energy and being around him. I loved our talks, listening to him, and being his friend. I missed him when he suddenly left my life.

He hugs me to him really hard and slaps my back. "Fo sho, *chica*! That's why I came today when Soli called me last week. I recently met

Felicia, a girl at my optometrist's office. She sees me and treats me like a guy, and she's a writer, like me." He adjusts his purple-tinted sunglasses and lets out a shining smile. "We really hit it off. Finally, after Dori, I meet someone who totally gets me. Soli said I could bring friends. I came early to help. Felicia's working, but she'll be here later."

"That's fantastic!" I feel relieved and a little sad—I'm not sure why—but I'm glad we can stay friends.

Tazer confides in me, "You know, when Francisco came into the picture, he became my competition."

"You're such a testosterone king!" I laugh, and the sadness leaps right out of me.

"The truth is that once I got to know you, I couldn't help but love your sarcastic sense of humor, your playful personality, and your different way of thinking. You're not so bad on the eyes, either. And besides, you grew on me like fungus!" We laugh heartily. "But for my own selfish reasons, I didn't want you dating another guy.

I wanted to be the *only* guy you fell hard for." He looks toward the bananas and back to me. "I was ecstatic that you treated me with respect, like a boi and not a lesbian. I guess if you'd allowed it, I could've fallen in love with you."

Soli screams from indoors. "Yo, dildos, we need some help!"

Tazer slaps me a high five. "I'm over you, *chica*! Let's go!"

I pull on his streaked bangs. "You're all right, Tazer."

We walk indoors arm in arm, just goofing off.

I'd bought party hats, balloons, and recycled crepe paper strips to hang from the ceiling, along with games, gifts, and an organic guava-and-cream-cheese cake. Soli bought a Santa Barbara piñata that had a large red cape covered with fake pearls. Soli's superslick in her lime green spandex minidress, so short and so tight you'd think she'll soon die of asphyxiation.

"Listen up, guys," she announces, tugging at her nose ring. "Once Mima pulls off the cape, little chocolate saints and teeny chocolate dicks will shower the floor."

We laugh hysterically. She's a total maniac!

The doorbell rings, and I let in the caterers. They leave globs of pink cheeses, *croqueticas*, greasy chicken wings, fried green triangular sandwiches, deep-fried glazed *churros*, ham-and-cheese balls, *empanadas de carne*, *papas rellenas* swimming in fat, neon orange pudding, *flan*, and custards. This is Soli's gift to her mom: clogged arteries.

I got an organic recipe book and made egg salad sandwiches, *bocaditos*, black bean hummus dip, and huge fruit bowls. Diego brought a truckload of chips and sodas. Tazer bought crates of organic juices, guacamole, crackers, and fancy food that I've never eaten, such as liver pâté and caviar. We're super-duper ready.

The phone rings, and I make a mad dash and answer it, in the privacy of Viva's bedroom. I shut the door behind me.

"Hello?"

"Laura?" Mami's voice is at the other end. I fumble and drop the phone. Then I pick it up with shaky hands. She must have gotten my phone message. I said I had changed and I wanted to introduce her to my new boyfriend. I waited a long time to let her know about Francisco. I needed to be certain that my relationship with him would work out. With Mami I must be completely sure she believes I've changed, or there's no going back home.

"Is everything okay?" I don't know what to expect.

"Not only did I get your message, but I know it's true about you dating a boy. Graciela recently told me she saw you with a tall, thin, dark-haired boy around Miami." She speaks fast Spanish, in a high-pitched voice, as if she were the happiest woman in town. "Is he *really* your boyfriend? You have a boyfriend, Laura? Tell me this is true!"

"Yeah, Mami. I do!"

Suddenly something inside me collapses, and I don't feel so blissful talking to Mami. I thought I'd be in paradise. The idea of her calling me back was so intense that I believed I'd be the happiest person alive. What a letdown.

She lets out a long sigh of relief. "Have you been seeing him a long time?"

I deepen my voice. "About five months." I want it to sound powerful, as if a century has passed.

"Five months! I can't tell you how happy I am!"

I play with the phone cord, feeling hurt that Mami hasn't even asked me how I'm doing. She hasn't a clue that I quit school or that I'm working full-time. All she gives a crap about is that I'm dating a guy. I should have known to expect this from her.

"That's the *best* news I've ever heard in my life!" She pauses a moment. What's his name?"

"Francisco Bustamante," I say dryly.

"*¡Qué cosa más grande la vida!* In Cuba the Bustamantes were wealthy, high-class people before Fidel, *el hijo de puta,* took their wealth and turned them into poverty-stricken animals."

I don't comment on Francisco's family not having been wealthy in Cuba, in case anything I say enrages Mami. I've learned my lesson. Being mute with Mami, never expressing my true feelings, and never saying the truth about things that will upset her is the best way.

"Listen, we finally moved into our dream house in Coconut Grove. We've just finished furnishing and unpacking. Osvaldo and I are leaving for Europe for three weeks the day after tomorrow. We'll be stopping in Spain to visit your aunt and uncle. I'll pick you up tomorrow at noon so we can talk."

"Great!" I can't wait to go to their new house and see Pedri. "Is Pedri going with you to Europe?"

"No. He'll be staying here with Zenaida. Osvaldo's sister adores him. She's become like a second mother to him. He doesn't want to go; he's terrified of flying and started having nightmares. I trust Zenaida to take care of him. You can come see him to make sure things are running smooth. If you're still changed and are still with your boyfriend, we can talk about your moving back when I return."

My hands get clammy, and I rub them on my

miniskirt. "Okay, Mami." She gives me the address of their new house, and I jot it down.

Pedri hadn't known how to explain where they were living. He'd just said, "It's no fun. I don't know nobody. There are no kids in the street to play with. It's bad. I miss my friends, and I miss you too much." I knew it was somewhere in the ritzy Coconut Grove neighborhood they'd been planning on moving to, but exactly where, I wasn't sure.

Suddenly my stomach feels as if it's on fire. I almost wish I had never called her to tell her about Francisco. I want her to love me no matter what.

"Can I talk to Pedri?"

She hands him the phone. "Laury!" The tiny, candy-sweet voice at the other end lifts my spirits.

"Little Punk! I'm going to see you every day now. We're going to spend Thanksgiving, Christmas, and New Year's together!" Now I feel as if a party were going on inside me. "I'll be there early tomorrow morning. I can't *wait* to see you, my Little Punk!" My call to Mami was all worth it now.

"Yaaaaaay!" He cheers, and it melts my heart. Even though I've been seeing him a lot during lunch breaks, it's not the same as being with him every day.

"It's Viva's birthday party, so I need to go now. But I'll pass by Toys 'R' Us tomorrow morning after breakfast before Mami comes to pick me up to see you."

"Okay, Laury. I love you."

"I love you more than all the deserts, rivers, and even the moon, my Little Punk. I can't wait to see you."

"Me too." We throw each other kisses, and he hands the phone over to Mami.

"See how easy it would have been if you had taken my advice and dated a boy from the beginning?"

I say nothing. Mami just keeps stabbing my heart without even knowing it.

"Okay, Laura, I'll see you tomorrow. I've missed you, I love you, and I want you back."

I close my eyes and swallow a few times.

"Okay. Bye, Mami." We hang up. I've missed her so much, too, and I love her deeply; but I couldn't utter those three words. I don't trust her to not hurt me anymore.

I slap my face a bunch of times, take deep breaths, and walk slowly to the living room.

People pile in: Soli's friends from work, Viva's metaphysical friends, and the neighbors. It's jam-packed.

Jaylene walks in. "Laura!" She hugs me nice and hard. "You look fantastic, girl!" She turns to the wild-haired, cinnamon-colored girl with melancholy, poetic eyes who's standing on her right. "This is Gisela." She points to me. "And this is Laura, the greatest tree and landscape sketcher in the world."

"Hey, I know you from Cha-Cha's restaurant, remember?" Gisela says in a melodic voice. She's got on the same type of funky, thrift-shop clothes I'm wearing. Her checkered pants are green and brown. I'm wearing checkered aqua-and-sea green pants that I turned into a miniskirt. Her Indian print blouse is long and slinky. Mine is short, showing my belly button, with long loose sleeves—seventies style. We've got on the same type of square-toed ankle boots.

She locks her dreamy eyes on mine. "How's it going?"

I want to say, "Great now, since you've just made my day and my whole life." But instead I say, "Good." My heart is skipping beats. I don't know what I'm doing and I grab a vase from the coffee table and polish it with my hands.

Jaylene saves the day. "Gisela is Rosa's friend—you know, the girl I've been dating. She just graduated from high school, and she also loves foreign movies. Since you love Italian and all types of foreign films so much, I thought you'd want to meet her."

Just what I needed, the girl of my dreams to love foreign films, too, right after I told Mami I was straight.

I speak to her in the broken Italian that I've learned from a travel handbook and from watching Italian films. *"Come stai?"*

Her braces have made her teeny teeth so

perfectly lined up, you'd think the dentist chiseled them down just before she got here. *"Bene."* She smiles sweetly, and my insides go all mushy, like mashed potatoes with hot, liquid butter. "That's about all I know." She laughs and holds on to her colorful beaded necklace.

We start yacking a mile a minute about all the new and old Italian films we've seen and love. She loves Lina Wertmuller, Fellini, Antonioni, and other old-time directors just as much as I do.

Being around her slaps me into reality. I hear Pedri's little voice: "Laury, I love you."

Something inside me rattles. The vase slips out of my hand and shatters into a million pieces.

Jaylene, Gisela, and I start pushing the glass into a little pile with our shoes. I insist that I alone will pick it up.

As I'm about to head for a broom, Tazer comes around with his arm over the shoulder of a thin, long-haired girl. I guess it's Felicia. Tazer sings loudly to Jaylene, "Hey, Jay, what do you say? Can't get them both inside your o.j.?" They hug. "So glad you made it, doof!"

232

Jaylene slaps Tazer's back. "Yeah, poof!"

Tazer introduces Felicia to me. "My beautiful date."

"I've heard so many great things about you, Laura." She's got large teeth, a long face, and vibrant golden eyes.

"Thanks," I say. "Tazer told me about you, too." She seems really nice and very feminine looking, with a tight, silky, multicolored dress; high heels; makeup; and dangling earrings. She's right up Tazer's alley, that's for sure!

"Hey, where's Rosa?" Tazer's sparkling eyes roam around the duplex.

"She had to work late. She's coming later."

Tazer's eyebrows leap upward when he sees Gisela. "Hey, you're the waitress at Cha-Cha's. What's up?" They all start yapping away, and I send them outdoors. I need to clear my mind. I erase Gisela from my brain.

Just as I'm heading to get a broom, Soli comes over with one. "*¿Que pasó?*" She starts sweeping.

I tell her the entire conversation I had with Mami.

"Your mom's a nutcase. I wish you hadn't told her you were seeing Francisco. She should love you no matter what." Soli's right, and her words tear through me.

I change the subject. I don't want to feel pain.

"Listen, why is this party filled with gay girls? Are you getting back at me for the fight we had ten million years ago? I thought we were totally over that."

"Bro. Don't be ridiculous. I just keep meeting gay girls at work. That's why the millions of lesbos are here."

"Oh, I see. I guess straight people are too nerdy to like your haircuts, huh?" I nudge her in the ribs and wink. We laugh.

She kisses my cheek. "No one can pull the wool over your eyes, Looly, that's for sure. So, yeah. I've got an ulterior motive, but can you blame me?"

"You're too much, Hootchi Momma." I can't get mad at Soli anymore. She does crazy stuff because she loves me so much.

She sweeps everything into the bag, places it

on top of her CD player, and stands with one hand on her hip and the other holding the tip of the broom, peering into my eyes. "I saw the gleam in your eyes when you were talking to Gisela. It's the same type of shine you had with Marlena. Bro, give her a chance. You hardly ever feel that intense attraction. She's the type of girl to make love with, not to have sex with." She starts sweeping again.

I grab her arm. "She's totally not into makeup, perfume, or plastic shit. I bet she's 'green.' And she's into Italian and foreign movies, too." I talk low and let it pour out. "Being around her makes me want to fly. I feel like I'm going to hyperventilate or die or explode or something."

"Shit! Looly, it's about *damn* time." She musses my hair and kisses my cheek.

I lower my head. "But being with her will ruin my life. I can't live without Pedri anymore. I just can't. It's either Gisela or Pedri. You know girls come and go. Look at Tazer. You thought he was really into me. Now he's all riled up about Felicia." I take a deep breath and let out a long, slow exhale. "I need Pedri more than anything in the world, Soli."

I get a dustpan from the closet and place it on the floor. She sweeps the dust left from the glass pieces inside it with such a serious face that I think I've finally talked some sense into her. I pour the contents into the bag.

"It's so sad you can't follow your feelings cuz of your crazy neuro mom. I know how hard it is for you to live without Pedri. I hate your choice, but I guess I'm forced to understand."

"Jesus, Soli." I kiss the tip of her nose. "Thanks. Thanks so much." I feel such a sense of relief that Soli gets it and that she's not trying to change my mind.

With broom in hand, she walks away from me and comes back with a *limonada*.

"Cheers to our friendship. I'll miss you if your psycho mom takes you back. Here. It's organic. No alcohol, just like you love it. Lots of mint leaves, honey, and lemon."

I take a sip and hand it over to her. "I'll miss you, too. I love you, Soli."

She takes a mouthful. "I love you, too, Looly."

Soli grabs the bag filled with glass from on top of the CD player, throws it in the trash, stashes the broom in the closet, and goes to find Diego.

Music blasts. Elbows and hips are going this way and that. Everyone seems to be having fun. I must admit that I haven't even thought of Francisco for an instant. In a way, I'm glad he's not here.

Jaylene comes to me and we hang around, talking. "Fun party. It's like a lesbian bar in here."

"Yeah. Thank Soli for that."

Diego comes over. He talks about the new music videos and musicians as we watch Soli dance with Gisela, Felicia, and Tazer. I can hardly watch Gisela's movements; she's so delicious. I love the way she sways her large, rounded hips in that smooth, sensual way. I look away and hope Soli's telling Gisela I'm married with six kids and a husband on skid row.

Soli leaves to pick up Viva, and I dance up a storm with everyone *but* Gisela.

Everyone's chillin', eating, dancing, and getting

to know one another when we hear, *Bang! Bang! Bang!*

People in the backyard zoom through the back doors and we cram into the kitchen. I hear Viva's key in the door.

Adela, Viva, and Soli walk inside as we rush forward. "Surprise!"

"*¡Ay, Santa María madre de Dios!*" Viva cries out. I drape my arms around weepy Viva and give her a zillion kisses. She looks supercute in her flowered polyester pink-and-green dress and pink flip-flops. She checks out the piñata and pulls the cape. Down comes a shower of saints and teeny penises. "*¡Jesucristo!*" The candy flies all over the place, and everyone goes wild. Chispita runs to the treats and growls as if the saints were alive.

I put on a salsa tape—a mix of Olga Guillot, Santana, Celia Cruz, and Tito Puente—Viva's favorite. Hips are moving all over the place. Feet are going this way and that. People are twirling around and around. Soli pulls Diego by the suspenders to the dance floor. He looks like a gangsta mafioso with baggy pants, a tight pullover, and slicked-back hair. She presses herself against him so tightly, you'd have to peel her off him in order to unglue them.

Gisela comes around, and I walk the other way. She scares the living shit out of me.

A tiny old man with bushy gray hair and a big belly arrives. He's wearing a *sombrero de guano* and a *guayabera*.

Soli peels herself from Diego. "Mima, this is Diego's dad."

Viva turns rose red, as if she'd swallowed a beet and it's leaked inside her cheeks.

"Gabriel Eufemio." His eyes are glowing, as if he's seeing Cleopatra rise from a sarcophagus. "Pleased to meet you." Viva's face glows.

The party is faaabulous! I spend the rest of the night dancing with Viva and Gabriel. Jaylene, Tazer, and Rosa manage to keep Gisela company all night long. For once in my life I believe I'm headed in the right direction.

Stinkin' Liar

Beep-beep-beeeeeeeeeeeeeeeeeep! Beep-beep-beeeeeeeeeeeeeeeeeeeeep!

I hop out of the hammock, place the bowl with my banana-oatmeal-nut breakfast on the ground, and run like a madwoman to Mami's new, glue-scented green Jaguar, leaving Chispita in the fenced-in backyard.

"Mami!" I lean into the driver's seat and kiss her cheek. She hugs my face hard to hers and kisses it many, many times. She smells familiar, like home. Tears stream down our faces. I look away, trying not to show too much emotion.

"I couldn't wait to see you and came early to

pick you up. Let's go." She wipes her tears with the back of her hand.

"Get out a minute; there's no one home." I want her to see how I live.

"Your neighbor," she says, still sitting inside the car, "the one that looks like a criminal, with the Santa Barbara tattoo, was eyeing my Rolex. I took it off and stuck it in my purse."

"Babalao Carasco is a nice guy, Mami." I roll my eyes.

Babalao Carasco is a santero. Although he's a cool neighbor, he kills poor, innocent roosters and goats to sacrifice them to the orishas when cleansing people of their ailments.

Mami continues to complain. "Only you, Laura Sofía Lorena, would choose to live in a Marielito *barrio*. Fidel, *el hijo de puta,* opened the doors to jailed criminals and they all moved *here*."

I love this *barrio*, close to my old *barrio*. And besides, it's not like I had a huge choice of places to go when she kicked me to the curb. But I don't say a peep.

I swing open the front door and Mami bolts through it, speaking *factoría* Spanish. Words fly around at ten miles a minute as she rearranges our furniture. "*This* chair doesn't match *this* wall." She shoves the kitchenette table away from the middle of the dining area and closer to the wall. She takes down my two framed paintings of the Cuban mountainside. "*Ay*, I don't know why you paint *la jungla cubana* when you can fill your walls with colorful art. All this brown and green will make you depressed."

"I *like* brown and green, Mami." I walk behind her, trying to grab my framed paintings from her. She darts and shoves me aside with her super-duper BIG beach ball butt.

She hangs my Cuba paintings in our bathroom, over the toilet bowl, on two of the four lined-up empty towel hooks.

"Want some yogurt?" I ask in an attempt to get her to calm down.

"*¿Estás loca?* I weigh one hundred and ninety-nine pounds. I'm going on a *caldo* diet until I lose fifty pounds."

"Mami, you're forty-nine! You can't live on broth."

"Forty-five! And if *that* doesn't work, I'm going to have to start eating air to lose weight."

I laugh and stuff a spoonful of yogurt in my mouth. "Eat more veggies." In some ways I'm glad it's the same old Mami in front of me. She's hilarious and tons of fun, except for her homophobic stuff. If I could just peel off the homophobia, she'd be the flyest mom in the universe to chill with.

"Vegetables give me a hernia."

"Veggies have nothing to do with a hernia, Mami." She continues to move things around as if it were her own home and as if nothing terrible had ever come between us.

"Your grandfather died of diverticulosis. I can't eat tomatoes or lettuce or anything with skin on it. I inherited that illness."

"Right, Mami." I raise my eyes to the ceiling.

"I just got my cholesterol checked, and it's a perfect two hundred and fifty without my ever having eaten a *single* vegetable."

"Two hundred and fifty!" I cough up a storm, and I nearly choke.

"*¡Ave María Purísima!* Laura! That's *normal* for a forty-two-year-old, my doctor told me."

"A minute ago you were forty-five. *What* doctor?"

"Dr. Benítez."

"Mami, Dr. Benítez is three hundred years old!"

"He was the greatest doctor in Cuba. All my friends go to him. He's giving me a face-lift."

"A *face*-lift? *Him*? Mami, *por favor*, don't get a face-lift from *him*. By now he can't even hold his ding-dong to pee."

"Don't worry. I know what I'm doing. My friend Sylvina just got a face-lift from him and now she looks *exactly* like a twenty-something Liz Taylor."

"Oh, my God, Mami! That's terrible. She used to look like a young J-Lo." I wash the empty yogurt container and throw it in the recycle bin, then sit on top of the kitchen table, swinging my legs. She throws herself on the couch and, *poooooof*, the air slowly comes out of it. "When's the operation?"

"*El mes que viene*. When I get back from Europe."

"Next *month*?" My stomach does cartwheels.

"*Ay*, Laura Sofía Lorena, you worry about *every*thing. You're too sensitive, just like Papi was."

"Mami, nurses have to tie you up with ropes when they give you shots. I can't believe you're going to let someone give you a face-lift. Your face is beautiful."

And it's true. Mami has gorgeous, thick, slanted, dark eyebrows and large almond-shaped eyes with long lashes. Her teeth are whiter than white and straight. She's got a killer smile with two dimples. She could be a face model for soaps, creams, and toothpastes.

"When you get to be forty and you start sagging, you'll tell me a different story."

"So, who do you want to look like?" I'm intrigued.

"An extremely young Sofía Loren." She pats

her face with both hands. "I named you after her, you know, my favorite movie star." Then she weirds me out even more. "I've been on a high-sugar diet. Sugar eliminates wrinkles."

"*What?*"

"*Sí*, Laura Sofía Lorena. Your body needs sugar or you go into a coma."

"That's wacked! Where'd you get *that* from, *Hola* magazine? Mami, won't you *ever* listen to me and eat some veggies?"

"I'm your mother. *You* have to listen to *me*!"

Loud, bouncy music sweeps into the duplex through the open windows. She stands abruptly and looks out into the backyard.

Our neighbor Maribel is dancing around to salsa music, getting her high heels stuck in the earth as she hangs clothes on the line and fastens them with clothespins. Her parrot, Chuchito, is flying around the backyard, squawking, "*¡Ay, Miguel! ¡Miguel!*"

Miguel's friends are standing around him, drinking beer and barbecuing. They laugh their heads off. "*Oye*, Chuchito's been listening to you and Maribel doing the *fuiqui-fuiqui*, eh?"

Mami pulls me by the arm. "What a *barrio*! *Ay*. To think I used to live like this. Come on! Let's go to my new house. Pedri is home, and Osvaldo and his sister are in the pool."

"First take me to buy Pedri some toys. I promised him."

"Later! We'll all go together. That way he can choose what he wants."

We climb into her shiny car; and in a heartbeat we're in Mami's fancy new two-story house in Coconut Grove.

After Pedri shows me all his new toys, I slide a bathing suit on him and off he goes to the pool. Mami gives me a tour around the spacious, all-white house; then she starts packing for her trip.

I open the sliding glass doors. An early September storm zoomed in this morning and cleared the bumpy black sky of clouds. I take a whiff of the salty, green, and flowery smells, and I almost feel whole again. I look toward the canal to check for the manatees that Pedri says look like cuddly baby elephants from afar. I can't *wait* to go down there and see them up close. Pedri said one almost got hurt by a motorboat yesterday. People just don't care.

The manatees are nowhere in sight.

I walk into the huge kitchen, done all in white tile and stainless steel. Mami sticks her head inside the refrigerator and picks at leftover flan. With my thumb and index fingers, I flick her big bootie two times, really fast. "Flan is excellent for losing weight, Mami." She lets out a cool laugh that permeates the house. It fills me with happiness that she's back to laughing with me.

We climb up the winding marble staircase, go out to the second-floor balcony, and sit on rockers facing the bay. Warm, mild breezes gently sway the Alexandra palms.

Without warning, flashes of Gisela's face fill my mind. I shut my eyes and push my thoughts away to a place from which I hope they never resurface.

I look downstairs and hear a loud *sploosh-oosh* as Pedri dives into the Olympic-sized pool. I wave to him. "Supercool dive, Little Punk!" My heart feels full again.

He waves back. "Laury, I did it!" He blows me kisses, and I give him a thumbs-up. He's chillin' with Zenaida, Osvaldo's cute and round-as-a truck-tire sister. She doesn't take her eyes off Pedri for one second. Even though she's not old at all, she looks like a funny old lady in her flowered, one-piece bathing suit and green rubber shower cap.

Mami's husband Osvaldo—tall, blondish, and well built—is sitting on the pool steps with his hairy white legs halfway in the water, having a drink. I can tell that he loves Mami and Pedri a lot, and I'm superpsyched about that.

I sit on Mami's lap, kiss her cheek, and press my cheek against hers. She kisses me back. "*Ay*, Laura Sofía Lorena." Just as I think she's going to be sweet and affectionate, like she used to be before the Incident, she says, "You've put me through such hell. Every day I prayed that you'd call to tell me you'd changed and to let me know who the degenerate girl was. But you didn't. You protected her and loved her more than your own family."

I have an instant, gut-wrenching reaction, as if a horse kicked me in the stomach. I quickly sit back on my rocker.

We rock for a little while in silence.

I wish I could tell her about the deep love I shared with Marlena and the pain I felt after our breakup. I wish I could talk about everything *I've* been through and everything she put *me* through, but that would make things worse. Isn't that what mothers are supposed to be for—for talking about important things? But since she thinks I'm at fault and I can't talk to her about my life, I change the subject before she becomes enraged; I talk about Osvaldo.

"Do you love him?"

She glances up but avoids eye contact. "*Of course* I love him. I would *never* marry a man I didn't love. You know, when Papi died and left us without a penny, I took on three jobs, sewing coats in *factorías* for rich gringos. For years I didn't have a life. I will never forget your papi. But now I'm starting to live and love again."

I want to make her laugh. She always gets sad when she talks about the past.

"Remember when I was little? One day you told me, 'Laurita Sofía Lorena, you have a cold. If you put *one* foot on the porch, you're going to get it.' But I did it anyway." Mami laughs up a storm, remembering. "You ran after me. I kept screaming, 'Mami, I didn't put a *foot* on the porch, just a *toe*!'"

"You've always had a strong personality, Laura." She chews the inside of her cheeks.

"I wonder who I inherited it from," I tease.

"*Definitely* not me!" She smiles, and her eyes glow. "Ask my friends; they'll tell you I'm *suave y dulce*."

"If your friends think *you're* soft and sweet, they're totally on drugs."

She lets out a big, colorful laugh, like the splashes of waves Pedri makes when he dives into the pool. I love it when Mami laughs; it makes me feel that maybe she still loves me.

"*¡Ave María!*" She points to a neighbor tanning

in her backyard in a bikini. "Skin and bones. And you"—she pinches my stomach—"you're slender because you came out like Papi's side of the family."

Mami yacks about how fashionable I look in my red stretch shorts and matching top. She talks about everything except real stuff. She can't handle anything deep. She starts yapping about buying this and that so she can keep decorating the new house. The only thing I'd buy if I could would be understanding. I'd take it by the hand and bring it right here and sit it next to Mami.

She changes the subject from buying things to me.

"You have the figure of a professional dancer or a model, but you chose a man's job—planting trees. *Ay*, Laura Sofía Lorena. If I had known you were going to turn out this way."

She searches her dress pocket for diet watermelon bubble gum, unwraps two pieces, throws me one, and sticks one in her mouth.

I chew fast, blow bubbles, and smack them shut inside my mouth.

252

She looks down at her long, freshly painted fuchsia fingernails. I almost blurt out something about Francisco, but it seems neither of us wants to bring up the topic. Maybe she's scared of what I'll say.

I play with the tips of my hair.

She stands abruptly. "*¡Ay, madre mía!* I forgot that while I was cleaning out my closet before moving, I found a coat I used to use when I was skinny."

"And when was *that*, Mami Pastrami with the big culiwami? When you were in Abuelita's womb?'

"*¡Tu madre!*" She laughs her head off as she wiggles her middle finger in the air. I kiss both her cheeks, and she kisses mine back. What a great feeling to have Mami goofing with me again. My smile barely fits in my face.

We walk downstairs and step onto white marble floors into the colossal living room. Mami rushes into her bedroom. I look around me. One wall is filled with wall-to-wall mirrors. On the rest of the stark white walls hang expensive, colorful modern paintings with detailed, thick golden frames. There's a white shag rug under an antique coffee table. In every corner there are tall, green, exotic plants.

I plop down on the plastic-covered peach velvet love seat. In a heartbeat she's back, carrying a bulky coat, which she tries to force me to try on. "Winters are getting colder in Miami. Last year it went down to thirty degrees. You *have* to be prepared."

"That coat's for Alaska. Not now, Mami. Later."

"*¡Ave María!* You were born with your hand up in the air, saying, 'Wait a minute!'"

"I'm not going to try this coat on now; it's one hundred degrees out! Later. I promise."

She plunks on the love seat, grabs my hand, pulls me to her, takes a container of pins out of her purse, and lifts up the coat. "Remember when Papi bought it for me in New York?"

I remember clearly. Mami, Pedri, and I used to hop on a train every summer to visit Papi when he worked as a horse groom in New Jersey at

Monmouth Park racetrack.

Mami and I have trouble talking about Papi without breaking down, but we try.

"Of *course* I remember this coat." I hold it in my arms, bury my face in it, and inhale all the memories of Papi. I couldn't have had a better father. There was no dad in the world as sweet and kind as mine.

I try on the coat, and it's a bit large on the sides. Mami has me stand in front of her, with my arms spread out. She sticks pins all the way from under the arms to the hem. I feel a need to blurt out something about Francisco, to jump-start the conversation, to get it out of the way, but I can't.

Even though the central air is on, beads of sweat drip down my eyebrows. The thick, fuzzy black coat is making me itchy, but I don't take it off. I need it on me. I need the memories of Papi's love around me. If Papi were still alive, I bet I could talk to him about everything.

Mami's eyes are watery. "Papi was so good to me and to all of you. Remember when he used to carry you, and lift you up in the air, and sing, '¡La *chiquitica más linda del mundo!'"*

Mami tries hard not to cry when she says Papi's words—"The prettiest little girl in the world!"—but tears stream down her face anyway.

I feel as if I've swallowed a baseball and it got stuck in my throat. Everything I've lost flashes in front of my eyes: Papi, Marlena, my reputation, Mami, my friends, my school, my old *barrio*.

I want to console Mami, but instead I ask her if she has ice cream.

"There's *mamey* ice cream in the freezer."

"Want some?" It's my best effort at making her feel good, even though I'm adding to the expansion of her two-ton bootie.

"*Sí.*"

I take off the coat carefully and give it to her. I scoop the ice cream into two white porcelain bowls and hand her one. I plunk down next to her on the love seat, hoping we can slowly build a bond of closeness and love again. I just have to be perfect and try not to ever upset her or say anything about my *real* feelings.

She devours her ice cream, scrapes the last

drop from the bowl, and licks the spoon. "Ahhh, I'm going to open a can of chicken broth and heat it up for dinner. I can't keep eating like this." She goes to the sink and washes our bowls.

I bite my nails, thinking that soon one of us will need to bring up the conversation about me being completely changed and in love with Francisco. I'm scared of Mami's reactions. We're getting along so well, I don't want to spoil anything.

Mami comes back. We talk about what color she wants me to paint a fruit tree mural on one of the walls in her bathroom. "Pastel yellow and salmon," I say.

"¡Qué *horrible!* That's the color of monkey shit and diarrhea. Neon orange is the 'in' color. You *have* to paint the fruits bright orange, with many hanging *mandarinas*."

I agree, just because I'm about to explode. I can't keep it in any longer. Without thinking I blurt, "I'm trying to fall in love with Francisco, Mami."

Her mouth drops open and her eyes widen.

"Trying? You mean you *haven't* changed?"

"No. No. That's not what I meant at all." My heart is pounding hard. I look out the glass doors toward Pedri and then back into her eyes.

She arches her eyebrows. "Then what *did* you mean?" She breathes fast and heavy. "You've been with him five months. You're either *in* love with him or *not*, but *trying* isn't good enough. Which one is it?" Without giving me a chance to speak, she says, "Tell me *once* and for *all* if you've really changed or not."

"Of course, Mami. I wouldn't be here if I hadn't." I should have known better. What an idiot I am to not have worded things perfectly to her satisfaction. One more slip and I'm a goner. Things were going so great. I'm stupid, stupid, stupid!

"So what did you mean about *trying* to fall in love with him?" She doesn't get off the friggin' subject.

"What I mean is that I'm *falling* in love with him." I say plastic, stupid things I know she'd love to hear. "You should see him, Mami; he's six feet five inches. One whole foot taller than me. He's so gorgeous in a skinny, model type way. His muscles pop out all over the place. He's kind of like a thin, strong, young Tarzan. You'll love him."

Mami doesn't give two cucumbers if a guy has a brain. She just cares about me being with a guy and that he's macho and good-looking so our kids will be gorgeous. She still hasn't asked me a thing about my life. She wouldn't even care that I dropped out of school as long as I'm on the "decent" road to getting married and having kids.

She smiles big. "Oh, well, then, that's fantastic, Laura. He sounds like a hunk who just needs a little fattening up. Don't you worry about that. Bring him here for dinner every night after we get back from Europe, and soon he'll have pecs to die for." Her smile fades away. "I'm sorry to tell you that I can't have you back until I'm *absolutely* sure you've changed. I can't go through the pain and humiliation you put me through again, especially not in front of

Osvaldo. He can never find out."

My heart drops in my chest. I look to Pedri and wonder how he'll take the bad news.

Mami keeps on. "I told everyone you're living at the house of a friend whose mother is really sick. I said you take care of her every day after school, for pay. Our family, friends, and new neighbors all think you're very responsible. Don't you *dare* tell them otherwise."

I stay quiet.

"Right now your feelings for Francisco are iffy. While living here you can't go back to immoral behavior." She repeats, "The day you move here is the day you're *absolutely sure* you're in love with a boy." She shakes her head. "Tell me more about Francisco."

I stay far away from my feelings of hurt and disappointment in order to not get her riled. I talk about Francisco, how I met him at a disco, and how he has a few acne scars that I think makes his features interesting in a rugged, macho way. All the stuff she wants to hear. I leave out that the disco was Papaya's and that whenever Francisco kisses me, I think about Gisela. She obviously wants a stinkin' liar for a daughter. And that's what she's getting. A big, fat, stinkin' liar!

Inside Out,
Upside Down

Every weekday these past two months I've spent chillin' with my little bro after work. We're both sad that Mami's taking so long to ask me back but happy to see each other so much.

Mami came back from her vacation, and Francisco has joined us for dinners every weekend at her house. Osvaldo is a friendly and sweet man. He has never asked me a single personal question. He couldn't give a rolling tomato about what I do for a living, or where I live. He just yacks and yacks about his boring businesses, or he tells a few jokes.

Mami adores Francisco, but no matter how hard I try to make her believe I'm in love with him, she tells me, "I *know* you're not." I think she's waiting till Francisco asks me to marry him and I say yes. Either that or she wants to test me for another one hundred years to make sure I'm totally straight. I guess she smells that something still isn't quite right. And it's true. My head is somewhere else, lost in the flowering bushes, thinking about Gisela. No matter how hard I try, I can't get her out of my mind. If I keep daydreaming about her, I may never pass Mami's sniff test.

I'm still living at Soli's. I spend weekend mornings with Pedri and Viva at museums or at the beach and weekend nights after dinner at my mom's, or kickin' it with Francisco, Soli, Diego, Tazer, and Felicia. Sometimes I chill with Tazer at his house. We've become even greater friends. He understands that I can't be seen alone with him out in the real world, especially not now. If Mami finds out, she definitely will *never* let me move back in.

Around Francisco my emotions are like April: never too hot, too humid, or too cold. Physically, though, I've recently been like June: hot, hot, hot! He's always like July: scorching! I told him to chill, to be cool like this month, November; and he promised he would.

Francisco and I made a dinner date. We finished eating a meal that his mom prepared: lentils and rice, tomato-and-onion salad, and *yuca con mojo*. I thank his cute, frumpy mother as I finish helping her clean the table. "*Gracias*, Fina. It was delicious."

"Anytime, *mijita*." She kisses my cheek.

I love Francisco's mom. For being Cuban, she's so mellow. She hangs out at home in housedresses, painting neighbors' nails. She takes care of her kids, and she doesn't miss a Cuban soap opera on TV. Their little apartment is impeccable, and she's always doting on Francisco and his brothers.

Francisco takes me to the backyard shack he just turned into his bedroom; it's a cement room with tall ceilings and hanging black-light lava lamps. The walls are painted deep purple. The only furniture is a velvety black armchair in front of a stereo system next to his bed and a little fridge where he keeps beer. There's a guitar in its case standing along a wall, and a bunch of *claves*, *timbales*, *tumbadoras*, and little bongos are littered all over the room. He's really into playing music. I love that.

On the wall I see his favorite photograph of his santero dad standing next to friends in Cuba and wearing a white *guayabera*, white baggy pants, and tons of white beads around his neck. Next to him are pictures of Francisco and me.

I smile. "Cool the way you made this into your new room."

"It's coming along." He grabs a beer from the fridge and slides on a CD. Soft *son* music comes on.

It started getting hot and heavy last month. Recently my body's had an urge to go all the way. I almost lost my head yesterday, but a voice inside snapped me back into reality: "You're not in love!" I must admit that I have a great time exploring his body, but it's frustrating that I can't feel emotionally close to him. Just knowing we can't be tight in that deep, intense way leaves me feeling extremely empty and lonely.

I lean against the open window and look outside toward the cages filled with colorful cockatoos—the birds his older brother sells for a living. He holds me by my shoulders and peers into my eyes. "Listen to what I've got to say."

My heart thumps fast. "What?"

He's got a glow in his eyes that speaks loud and clear. "I want you to be my girl and only mine."

I zip up my jean jacket, clear my throat, and look deeply into his eyes. "But I'm not seeing anybody else."

He takes a swig of the beer. "Why can't you answer about being only mine?"

"Isn't my answer enough?"

"No! I want you to tell me you're madly in love with me like you were with Mario. I want to hear that you're *all* mine. Haven't you forgotten him yet? Is that it?"

I told him about "Mario" when he asked about my ex. I couldn't bring myself to tell him the whole truth.

"It's not Mario. I just think I can never fall in love again." I remember how it used to be with Marlena before everything slid down the edge. Nothing with Francisco comes remotely close to what I felt for her.

He bites his thick bottom lip. "That's crazy. Why can't you love me like you loved that fucking Mario guy? What, did he have a bigger *chorizo*?"

My heart pounds in my chest at his unexpected anger and his disgusting response.

"Maybe you should be dating other girls. If you want, we can be just friends." I can't force my heart anymore. I've been trying too hard, for too long.

"Don't be ridiculous." He sucks on his beer. "I hate this Mario guy. He's ruined you."

He had to mess up everything by mentioning "Mario." I wish he didn't have to bring this up; it just reminds me of the lie I've been telling him.

He takes my face, brings it closer to his, and kisses me. His nubs chafe my skin, and I hate the feeling. He's a great kisser when we're rolling around in bed but way too harsh when I just want to feel emotionally close and not sexual.

Suddenly, kissing him is making me feel lonelier than I've ever felt in my life.

There's a dark hole deep, deep in my heart that's like a painful wound. I can't help it, and tears begin to drip down from my eyes.

He takes his lips off of mine. "Hey, what happened?"

"I'm trying to fall in love again, Francisco, and it's just not happening." I'm as honest as I can be. "I don't want to hurt your feelings." I can't tell him that I miss the closeness of being with, and kissing, a girl.

"You'll fall in love with me. It takes time. You'll see." He kisses me deeper and harder.

Maybe I will. Maybe feeling more alone the more time I spend with him is all worth it. I finally have my family back.

I stop kissing him and grab the beer from his hand. "Why do you always have to be drinking? It's disgusting."

He snatches the bottle from me, guzzles the beer, and throws the bottles in the trash bin. "A few beers is no big deal." He drops his husky voice to a whisper. "Maybe when we go all the way you'll fall in love with me. But I'm glad you don't ever want to go all the way."

"Why?" I'm confused.

He tilts his head to the right, and his long, black hair falls over his left eye. "I want the girl I marry to be a virgin, to be mine and just mine. If we'd have done it, I wouldn't respect you or be serious about you."

"You're weird." He's just like every other Cuban guy. They want to possess us, for us to be virginal and virgins. But look who's talking. I used to feel that way about Marlena. I loved that I had been her first and only one. We honestly felt like one, like we belonged to each other.

He kisses my cheek, goes into his pocket, takes out a little black velvet box, and hands it to me.

I open it slowly. It's a little Cuban coin hanging on a silk string that matches the one I gave him. "Beautiful!" I'm glad the conversation is going in a different direction. I put the necklace around my neck, fasten the clasp securely, and feel the coin with my fingers. I love everything Cuban.

He lets out a sweet laugh, throws the gift box in the trash, and rubs his hands together. "I have secret ways of making you fall in love with me and marrying me. A guy can't wait *that* long."

I give up trying to break up with Francisco. I must continue trying to fall in love with him. I throw myself on the cushiony armchair and sink into it.

The slow dance music is still on in the background. He tears off his leather jacket, throws it on the bed, walks to me, and pulls me to him. I allow myself to be taken into his arms and rest my face on his chest. He smells salty. He's a good dancer, a soft mover.

From the half-open windows come soft sounds of bamboo chimes and wind-bells. I feel his heartbeat on my face becoming stronger and stronger. Before I know it, he's whispering into my ear, "I want you." His lips come close to mine, and he finally gives me a soft, passionate kiss.

I feel my body wanting more. I squeeze him to me, and I get into the rhythm of kissing. I bite his lips and taste all of him. Our lips are locked in a smooth dance; but then he kisses me hard, and I fall, fall, fall out of desire.

I stare out the window at blazing stars, wondering if I'll ever feel close to him or if it will always be *just* physical.

I'm dizzy with thoughts crowding my brain. Maybe I should tell him about Marlena now and get it over and done with.

I slam on the brakes and separate myself from him. "I've got to tell you something."

I feel all shaky inside.

"What?"

My heart bangs in my chest something fierce. "Uh . . . nothing. I've just gotta get going."

"No, tell me. Tell me. What's going on?"

"Nothing, nothing. It was stupid anyways."

He gently grabs my hands. "I'm not letting you go till you tell me."

"Jesus! I told you it's no big deal." I pinch his rock-hard stomach. "It's just that I wanted to thank you again for the gift. That's all. Really. I've gotta get going."

"What's *wrong* with you? Stay a little longer. Come on. We can go dancing at a club or see a movie. Don't be that way," he pleads.

"I don't want to go out tonight. I've got to feed Chispita and walk her, then I'm going straight to sleep. I'm tired." I'm being a pain. I'm surprised he isn't sending me to hell, but I realize I *have* to put an end to this relationship no matter how much I enjoy fooling around with him.

"Listen," I go on. "We can't continue being together. Let's just be friends. You're a great guy; but you're moving too fast, and my heart isn't keeping up."

"Too fast?" He lets out a dramatic laugh. "Don't be silly. You're just the sensitive type. I know you'll fall in love with me in time. Chill.

We're staying together."

It's as if he's not listening or he doesn't care. "No! We need to end it now and become just friends."

"Don't be crazy. Virgins are so damned emotional, man. Trust me. You'll fall in love with me. I've been in your shoes. Just give it more time. I'm not letting you go. I'm in love with you."

Those words give me a jolt. "No, Francisco. It's not fair to you if I keep this up."

He points to his big banana. "No worries! *I'll* keep *this* up for both of us!" He laughs his balls off.

"You're not listening!"

"Well, if we're *just* friends, then I'll come over to Soli's and we can play computer games."

"Why aren't you taking me seriously?"

"We've been through this so many times." He kisses my lips. "Okay. Okay. Go ahead. Go home. I'll see you tomorrow."

"No, Francisco. This time it's for real! We're just friends, okay?"

"Sure, sure. *Best* of friends." He kisses my

cheek. "Ride safely."

I put on my helmet, grab the handlebars, hop on my bike, and ride into the silvery night, not knowing which way is up or which way is down.

Untangling

'm riding home from Francisco's place, poking my thoughts around, digging for ideas about how to give Mami the news about the breakup. All I'm coming up with is a big, black blank.

I put my feet to the pedals and ride through the *barrio* in which I grew up. I find our old home and park across the street from it, at the shoe factory, and stare at the front yard. I see myself as a little kid playing slip 'n slide with Gloria, my good friend who lived next door. I recall us laughing like hyenas at every little thing.

I rode my bike here last month so I could see

my old *barrio* friends. That was the craziest thing I could have ever done.

I knock on Gloria's front door. Her mother answers. "Never set foot in here again. My daughter will grow up to get married and have children as God intended for girls." She stabs my heart. "I'll pray to God that he straightens your path. You're a closed chapter in Gloria's book. As for Gloria, she isn't allowed to speak with you again. Don't ever come or call here."

She slams the door in my face. I gulp down my tears.

I get home and tell Soli what happened. Soli confides in me, "The night your mom kicked you out, I heard through the grapevine that somebody left an anonymous letter at your front door. It said you couldn't go to any of your

neighbors' houses anymore cuz
their children 'need to be protected
from filth.' They signed their
names with Xs. Your neuro mom
had a fit."

I can't bear the memories. I feel as if I'm blind-folded, riding through a dark tunnel in search of light. Out of nowhere a taxi hits the back wheel of my bike.

Bang! Crash!

The bike is skidding out of control. I can't stop it! It's spinning around and around and it slides into a sidewalk and, *wham!*, I hit a post. I'm on the ground, holding my aching stomach, feeling like throwing up. I look at my arms and body. I'm still alive and in one piece. There's blood on my left shoulder where my jacket was torn. I cover my eyes with my arm.

The passenger in the taxi runs to me. "You okay?"

"My shoulder," I answer, looking up at him.

"Don't worry. I called 911. That idiotic driver

almost ran you over!" He blinks nervously. "You're lucky you didn't get killed. Don't move. Stay put in case you've broken something."

In the emergency room I give the nurse my home number and she calls Soli and Viva. I don't feel like seeing Mami right now. She'll just give me crap about riding a bike late at night. I don't need the extra pressure. And besides, I don't want Pedri to worry.

I have a bandaged-up, scratched-up left shoulder, a bump on my left thigh, and a bunch of scratches and bruises on my legs. But I can move my left arm, and I didn't break anything. My bike is an accordion, though.

Soli speeds into the room like a locomotive, with a new guy, and Tazer trails behind them.

"Bro, what happened?" She kisses my forehead, uncovers me, and scrutinizes my body to make sure I'm okay. She takes my hand to her heart. "You all right?"

"I'm fine—just this." I shrug my bandaged shoulder.

Tazer kisses my cheek and searches my face. "You look like you're still in one piece." He covers me with the bed sheet.

Soli purses my lips together by holding my cheeks and smacks me a big one. *Muuua!* She faces the new guy with a gleam in her eye. "Paublo, this is Laura."

Soli's new guy is a husky, spiky-haired, dyed-blond, coffee-colored guy who wears all leather. He's got a goatee that makes him look like a motorcycle rider, a tongue ring, and two silver earring hoops. He's probably got tattoos on his arms.

"Hey, Laura," he whispers in a deep, sensual voice. "I met you at Viva's birthday party. Remember?"

"Yeah, hi." How could I forget Gorgeous Godzilla among a room full of girls?

"I've just stayed away. You know," he looks at Soli. "She was dating Diego." He smiles. "Can't wait till you get better so we can all kick it." He plants a kiss on my cheek. "Gotta use the bathroom. Be right back."

Tazer sits on the corner of my bed and just stares at me, as if I were a painting. He breathes in and lets go a big exhalation. I can tell he's relieved that nothing happened to me. He texts Felicia on his cell to let her know I'm okay.

"Isn't he *hot*? Looly, he's the *hottest* guy I've ever gone out with. Do I look good? Bro, look at me." Soli takes a spin, and her tight yellow-and-red spandex minidress sticks to her curves like a corset. Her big boobs spill out of the top like two cantaloupes. It could be snowing and she'd still be wearing her minidresses.

"You look like you just came from taking your first Holy Communion." She lifts her left eyebrow and releases a thunderous laugh. I throw her a piercing stare. "I can't believe you dumped Diego." I clear my throat. "I really liked him. Where'd you pick Paublo up, hustling on the street corner?" I'm pissed that she threw Diego away like an old rag. I know what *that's* like.

She whispers into my ear: "Diego dumped *me*, but I don't want to talk about it now. Later." Her voice rises. "Damn, Looly, I'm such a jerk. Here I am talking about *my* life, and *you* almost got killed. You okay? Is there anything I can get you?" I shake my head no. "I went to pick up Tazer as soon as I heard. If anything ever happened to you, I'd die. I mean it." Soli takes my hand and kisses it. Tears well up in her eyes. Mascara drips down her face, leaving long streaks. "I know I'm a pain, but I can't live without you. I'm so glad you're alive."

I pull her to me and kiss her cheek. "I can't live without you either, Hootchi Momma. You're my sister for life." And it's true. I can't imagine my life without Soli.

"When you coming back home?"

"Tomorrow. They want to keep me for observation cuz my head got slammed around a lot. My helmet's all banged up." I point to my cracked and warped helmet on the chair.

"Shit!" they both belt out.

There's a loud racket in the hall. Viva whizzes in like a tornado. Gabriel trails behind her.

"*Ay*, Laurita, thank all my *santos* you're alive!" She fills my face with *besitos*. "*¡Ave María*

Purísima! ¡Gracias, Dios!" She makes the sign of the cross on her chest. "I call your mami to tell her what happened. She not home. And the message machine is no working."

"I didn't want to tell her, Vivalini. I'm fine. Please don't call her again."

She hands me the cutest stuffed polka-dot elephant.

I kiss the tip of Viva's round nose. "What? They didn't have a stuffed saint?" I cuddle the smiley elephant in my arms.

Viva gives out a sweet belly laugh. "*Ay, Laurita* . . . you is always eating what the chickens nibble. When frogs grow hairs and birds grow teeth, you will estop being such a pain in the butt." Her tiny birdseed eyes slant. "The *elefantico* is Ganeshito, the Indian god who opens paths when they is closed."

Gabriel leans over and gives me a soft peck on the cheek. He winks at me and tells me in Spanish, "Glad you are okay, Laurita. If there is anything I can do for you, you let me know. Gabriel Eufemio Fernandez is here at your service."

I'm so glad he and Viva are together. He's got to be the sweetest little old man in the world. It's just strange that he's Diego's dad, and he'll soon meet Paublo. I hope he doesn't feel weird.

I take hold of his tubby little hand and squeeze it. "Thanks."

Viva can't keep her trap shut. "My goodness, Laurita, you is going to kill me of a heart attack. Don't drive a bicycle on the streets no more, *mijita*. You and Soli Luna never listen to me. *¡Ay, mi madre!* Is you feeling okay, Laurita?"

"I'll live." I give her a bunch of loud smoocheroonies on her cheeks. "My only problem is that I can't pinch your *culito* till my wrist and arm heal."

Viva points to the heavens. "This is a punishment from God. He no want you pinching my butt no more." I pinch her butt. *"¡Ay, Dios mío! ¡Santísimo sacramento!"* She looks up to the ceiling. "Thanks so much, my *espíritus y santos*, for not letting anything happen to my Laurita."

"I'm going to take you to Hollywood, Vivalini. You'll make Salma Hayek look like she needs acting classes."

Paublo comes back all smiles. He shakes everyone's hand as he's introduced as Soli's friend. I wonder if Gabriel knows that Diego broke it off with Soli. He must. He looks a little sad.

Francisco unexpectedly walks in with a hurried stride. "Viva called me and told me you were here. Are you okay?"

"Barely alive," I goof.

He hands me a bouquet of red roses. As he comes to kiss my lips, I gently turn my face and kiss his cheek. I know *exactly* where I'm headed, and I don't want to lead him on.

I take a whiff of the flowers and smile. "They're so pretty. Thanks."

Viva and Soli hug him. He shakes Tazer's and Gabriel's hands, and they pat each other on the back. He reaches Paublo. "Hey, Paublo, man, what's going on?"

Soli explains to us, "Either Francisco or I cut Paublo's hair, depending on who has fewer clients at the time." They all yack as Soli leans in to me and whispers in my ear, "I miss Diego so much."

I do to her what she did to me when I was missing Marlena at Papaya's. "Forget about him, girl. I'm taking you to a club so you can meet lots of other guys right away. No wonder you look like you're going to a funeral in that dress." I roll my eyes. "I didn't realize you were grieving."

She squeezes the tip of my nose. "Bro, you're such a dildo. I guess it's payback time, huh?" I nod.

I grab her hand and whisper to her, "Sorry, Soli. I know it sucks." She squeezes my hand.

Soli and Francisco talk about doing a girl's hairdo for her fifteenth birthday party. My mind drifts off to Soli's *quinces*.

"Remember when your mom spent her *entire* savings just to buy your gown?"

"*You* had a *quinces*?" Tazer slaps his thighs and laughs hysterically.

"Thanks a lot, bro," Soli complains, and lets go of my hand.

Tazer bugs her. "You don't look like the traditional type. You're just waaaaaay too cool for that."

"Well . . ." I keep talking even if Soli's going to

be really pissed at me. "A month later Soli wanted to burn her *quinces* photo album. She said, 'I'm sick and tired of Mima showing it around the *barrio*, at work, and to people she's never even met before.'" I put on my best impersonation of Soli and her lively, sexy voice. "'I'm going to burn those suckers to a crisp. Looly, I swear on all the saints that if any of my homies see these pictures, I'm going to *kill* myself. Mima won't find out. She thinks they're stashed away in the closet.' Remember, Soli?"

"How could I forget if you never let me forget?"

"I told Soli she was nuts to want to burn the pics. I said I'd keep them for her and one day, when we're *viejitas*, we'd crack up looking at them. But she wouldn't let me have them."

"I've gotta see them, please!" Paublo begs. "Where are they?"

"No way!" Soli booms.

Viva has on a wicked smile. "I show you. I keep them in a secret place at home."

"*Sí.*" Gabriel smiles. "She already showed me."

He kisses the tips of his fingers all at once. "Soli Luna looked glorious, like a saint in heaven."

I crack up at the thought of Soli with a halo around her head. She pinches my stomach and I smack her hand.

I go on. "That day Soli showed me the album and said, 'Looly, swear to me you'll *never, ever, ever* tell anyone you've seen these pics. If you do, I'll never talk to you again.' Remember, Soli?" I'm laughing.

"Yeah. You swore to *La Vírgen María,* Looly."

I look at Paublo. "Soli's *quinces* was the first in the history of our culture without teens. The only way she would have the party was if no one our age was invited. She told her mom, 'Mima, if you invite *any* of my friends, I swear to God I'll take off the gown and run away from home!'"

Soli and Viva laugh, remembering. "Yeah, the party was filled with Mima's adult *barrio* and work friends."

"But knowing Laura," Tazer says, "she just *had* to show up, right?"

"I like a good challenge," I admit. "She

banned me from her party, so what else could I do but show up? When she saw me, she yelled, 'Why'd you *do* this to me? Leave *now*! Don't look at me, I look like a clown in this dress!'"

We laugh like a bunch of loonies. Soli's good mood is back. "Hey. Remember your *quinces*?" She's trying to get back at me.

"Oh, God! Who could *ever* forget?" I don't mind talking about my tacky *quinces*.

"Her mom and uncles went into debt just to throw her a wild party." Soli puts her whole body into her explanation. "She was lowered from a helicopter into the street in front of her yard. Her ball gown was pink and ruffled, with sequins. It was *so* wide, she didn't fit through the front door. She had to be *pushed* inside!"

"That's true!" I crack up so much, tears splash my face.

Soli keeps on. "Her aunts, uncles, and cousins came from Hialeah and Spain, just for the event. Her uncle led her into a huge pink shell with fake pearls and sequins glued on it. Later on a white horse galloped in, and she sat on it for photographs!"

"What a scene that was!" I can't stop laughing.

"I'm glad my dad never made me change my ways and have me behave like a sissy Cuban girl," Tazer says. "I would've died if my dad had wanted me to have a *quinces*. Can you imagine me in a puffy *quinces* dress?" Everybody bursts out laughing. "But still, I'd love to see those pictures."

"Yeah!" Francisco and Paublo say.

For a moment there is silence. Viva holds on to Gabriel's hand with one hand. With a rosary in her other hand, she holds on to my right hand, praying silently over me. Soli sits on the bed holding my left hand. Tazer stares into my eyes and smiles, like only a good friend can. Francisco stands beside me. Paublo hangs around looking at me with a sweet face. He keeps asking me, "Sure you don't want anything? Any coffee or food from the cafeteria?" I guess he's a good guy after all.

Most of us have people in our lives who come and go; some are far in the distance and don't matter at all, but I've found a bunch that I can't live without. I look to Soli, Viva, Francisco, Gabriel, and Tazer. I kind of wish Diego were here, too. I feel a warm sensation in my stomach, like I used to feel when Papi hugged me. For a long time now people have hated me. These people love me and I love them back. In a strange way I feel renewed, like a huge change is coming, like I know I can make my life into something great.

Silence Shouts!

I t's a glisteningly bright November morning, but inside me it feels as if spring is bursting out in full bloom. I see it from every direction, leaping like a gazelle through the bushes in wild colors. The world around me smells like orange-and-mango fruit salad and tart green apples. I'm alive, and everything is beautiful. It seems like such a long time since I was suffering and confused. I'm sure my whole life is going to change for the better. I know exactly what I've got to do to make my life fantastic. And I'm going to get it done right away!

Today we're starting a large landscaping job at

a ritzy Miami Beach mansion. Paco forced me to take the week off to heal, and I did. I shopped around for a new bike and helmet. Paco wants me to be careful with my shoulder, so I'm going to sketch the back landscape while the crew works on the front yard.

Francisco decided to take his two-week vacation early, starting last week, thinking that he'd spend time with me at his place. Soli and the other haircutters split the customers he'd booked, and everyone gave him the thumbs-up. He didn't pay attention to what I'd said about us being just friends. When I wouldn't budge, he left with his uncle on a fishing trip to the Bahamas. His last words were "I'm not going to call you, so you can see how much you'll miss me. When I return, things will be back to normal and hotter than ever."

I get to work with a big, juicy grin, not having seen the crew since my accident. I hug everyone; but just as I'm about to hug Che, he pushes me away and glares at me with a strange look in his eyes.

I leave and park my new orange mountain bike with tall handlebars next to a tree.

Che comes to me and spits out, "You know Sandra Carasco?" My heart sinks.

"¡Hola!" Paco pulls up the driveway. I let out a sigh of relief. "Everybody get to work, except Laura." They leave, and I walk over to Paco and kiss his cheek. I want to thank him for saving my life, but I don't. Then he'll ask me what I mean and I could never, ever tell him.

We walk to the backyard. Paco takes out his thick, colorful plant, tree, and shrub book and leafs through it. I grab my sketch pad, charcoal, and colored pencils from inside my bag. "Our client wants shade, color, and many exotic palms in the front." He shows me pictures of the plants we can use. "Let's give them a Southern magnolia tree over there"—he points to the spot—"and a live oak north of it by the side of the house."

My heart is pounding fast, knowing what awaits me when I get back to Che. I nervously sketch the three-story mansion with shaky hands and paint the magnolia with large, heavily overlapping leaves and the live oak with tons of tiny leaves in vivid green.

I draw the outline of a stone path leading from the back porch to a pond surrounded by a semi-circular hedge of white gardenia plants. Overlooking the pond, I design a seating area with wooden benches.

To the left of the pond, I outline a tall trellis threaded with climbing red roses.

With large strokes I paint tall, skinny Alexandra palms in a row on one side of the pond and red salvia plants circling them.

I draw the exotic palms that Paco showed me in different locations. I fill in splashes of color by adding pink, orange, purple, and yellow flowers in circles all around the palms.

"¡*Maravilloso*, Laura!" Paco messes up my hair. "I'm off to show Chago. I'm taking Jaylene. She's a computer expert and knows how to place the sketch in the computer while Chago and I work out an estimate. Keep an eye on them so they don't slack off."

I walk him to his truck.

He calls to Jaylene with a whistle and a wave of his hand. They climb into his truck, and Paco looks into my eyes. "I wish Marlenita were here so she could see how outstanding you've become at drawing landscapes."

I'm too busy thinking of the question Che asked me to care about Paco's comment. My heart trembles. "Go water the plants. Don't do any digging or lifting today." He takes off.

I get to the front, and Che walks toward me in angry strides.

"Let's go to the back so we can talk in private." I follow him as he lights a cigarette.

He leans against the back porch. "Well, *do* you or *don't* you know Sandra Carasco?" His muscles tighten in his face and neck.

"Why?" I ask, knowing well what's coming. I can't believe Jaylene left with Paco. I know she'd help me out. Che knew Paco was taking off this morning. He really planned it well. What a creep.

He stands, puffing the cigarette right in front of my face. As I try to step away, he shoves me up against the porch. "You ain't moving from here, *lez*bo."

My knees tremble. "I, I . . . I need to get to work." I'm moving away when he stands practically on my feet. He stares me down, holds my arm tightly, and won't allow me to move. "So, *lez*bo. Know what I do to *lez*bians, huh?" I don't say a word. "Answer me!" His eyes are like gleaming daggers.

I stutter, "I . . . I . . . I don't know." My heart feels as if it's wobbling inside my chest.

He flicks and shoots the cigarette a few feet away from him, then slips out a pocketknife from his belt pocket. Sticking the point of the blade to my neck, he whispers, "I cut them up good."

I can't stop my body from shaking. Sweat drips off my forehead. I know I have to act or he'll hurt me. I kneel and beg, "Please, please don't hurt me."

"Hey, crew!" he yells in Spanish. His electrifying laughter fills the yard.

The crew runs to us with confusion in their eyes. "What's going on?"

I'm still in the kneeling position. "Look! I've

got her where I've *always* wanted her."

His squeals fill my brain, and it pisses me off. Even though his knife is still at my throat, I realize that he's not up for hurting me. He just wants to humiliate me in front of everyone.

"Put that knife away. Please." Camila looks horrified.

"Are you out of your mind?" El Tigre and George confront him, but he doesn't let go of the knife.

I carefully rise from my kneeling position and face Che. "Sicko."

He lets out a robust laugh and spews his vomit breath on me. "Think your little words will hurt me, dyke?" He presses the knife a little harder against my neck and I feel the pinch.

"No, but what *will* hurt you is when I call the police." I don't move a neck muscle as I speak. My face and shoulders are tense. "Everyone here is a witness."

"Yeah, *mano*! Put that knife down!" George demands.

El Tigre snorts. "I'll make sure you get jail time

if a *speck* of her skin is scraped off." His eyes become two large saucers. "Put that knife away if you know what's good for you, asshole!"

Che doesn't budge.

I let it out. "One drop of blood and it's jail time for you, punk-ass jerk. I hear they've got tasty food in the slammer, and I *know* how much you love butt sex." I don't hold my tongue, but I'm frozen stiff. One slight move and the knife will pierce my skin.

George yells, "She's serious, Che! Let go of that fucking knife!"

When he doesn't listen, El Tigre and George abruptly twist Che's arms till he drops the knife. Che doesn't fight back. He just chuckles like an idiot. El Tigre picks up the knife, puts it in his shirt pocket, and zips up his jacket. "You're not getting it back unless you want the cops here."

I let out a sigh of relief and turn to Che. "I'm calling the cops on Jaylene's cell as soon as she arrives." No punk-ass criminal is going to make me feel scared ever again. "Get out of my way!" I push him to the side and face the others. "Thanks, guys."

Che sees how serious I am and lets out a ridiculous laugh. "Hey, I was just joking!"

I stop in my tracks, turn around, and slowly walk to him. "Well, if that wasn't the *funniest* joke *ever*! Tell it to the cops when they arrive, asswipe. I'm sure they'll pee their pants."

His laughing stops cold. He crumples up his forehead. "In case you're wondering, Sandra is my cousin. She told me all about you yesterday, and I told the crew." He spits on the ground. "No *won*der you never looked at George, El Tigre, or me. And that Francisco guy is probably a fag acting like your boyfriend. We were all fooled. You're such a liar, making us believe you were one of us."

Everyone's attention zooms in on me.

Camila clears her throat. "We don't care, Che. Leave her alone. She's got her reasons for not having told us." I look at Camila, surprised.

Che doesn't listen. *"Tortillera de mierda,"* he mutters under his breath. "You should have told us you were one of those."

George cracks his knuckles really loudly. "She didn't have to tell us shit." He faces me. "You had us fooled, Laura." He lets out a vibrant laugh. "You sure look like a pretty girl, not like a bull-dyke or whatever they call themselves, like Jaylene and Tazer."

Che doesn't take his eyes off me. His ears and neck flush a bright red. "So suddenly all of you love queers and *tortilleras,* huh?" A thick bluish vein on his forehead pops out.

El Tigre is sucking on a toothpick. He spits it out and sneers, "Yeah, slime. You got a problem with *that*?"

The sun glares on Che's bloodshot eyes. In silence he stares at El Tigre, then at me. With cold hatred in his eyes, he says, "People like you are sick and abnormal!"

"Ab*normal*?" Something breaks inside me. "Ab*normal* is to hurt people just because they're different!" No one expects me to come on so strong. I look Che square in the eyes. "So *what* if I'm gay? At least I'm all about love, not hate!"

"Yeah, *comemierda,*" El Tigre agrees.

I go on with more power than ever. "You choose. Me calling the cops so you do jail time or you're fired." I point to the gate. "I don't give a flying butt hole what your choice is. Paco will find another helper just like *that*." I snap my fingers in his face and walk away.

George and El Tigre join me. Camila stays by herself and walks way behind us.

El Tigre lets out a fiery, energetic laugh. "We were shocked when Che came to us this morning, girl. Not in a billion light-years would we have thought you were gay. I never said a thing when he made those horrible remarks at Tazer's because I wanted no trouble. But I've had it up to *here*"—he grabs his nuts—"with that idiot. You can only take so much."

"That's for sure." I feel relieved that the crew isn't like Tazer thought. They're not so bad after all. They're intrigued about me having been with Francisco. I have a lot of explaining to do later.

Camila is off by herself. Maybe she'll come around. At least she's not being nasty, and she did stand up for me. I guess she's not comfortable around me after I said I was gay.

I get to the pile of coral rocks and look back at Che. He's standing around with a strange look on his face as if he's posing for a photograph. The friggin' coward.

I shout, "Leave or jail time!"

He storms out through the gates with his own hatred trailing behind him. He climbs into his truck, shoots us a bird, and drives away.

The days that I would have run after him are over.

Temptation

Last week when I fired Che, I had to face Paco. "Where's Che?" he asked. No one said a word. "He got pissed at me and left," I explained. The crew and I had a blast working together. Jaylene is thrilled that I'm gay. She won't stop talking about "queer" politics, which I don't know a flying fricassee about, but it's cool with me. Camila hasn't come around. She's still extremely quiet and keeps to herself. I hope that's just her way of being and nothing personal against me or gays. Che hasn't come back, and Paco replaced him with Elegio, a funny Nicaraguan guy who's round as a bowling ball.

Francisco arrived tanned and refreshed, and with a lot of shark tales. He called to tell me that he wasn't going to let me go so easily. "Give me one last chance for old time's sake," he pleaded. I let him know that we were definitely broken up but that I'd meet with him *only* as a friend, because I needed to come clean.

He's driving me to South Beach pier, with the Jeep windows open. It's freezing, and my nose and ears are numb; but the wind feels good on my face.

I tell Francisco that I have something important to tell him, but he insists, "We'll talk about everything later. Let's go for ice cream first, then dancing at Papaya's, where we first met."

There's nothing like ice cream on the most frigid day of the year.

He's also got something important to tell me, which makes me nervous. I suspect that he didn't take our breakup seriously and that he might propose to me, thinking that a marriage prospect will change my mind. He says a little dancing first will make everything easier.

I ask him, "Tell me now." But he won't. Francisco is that way. He likes things set a certain way, and he won't bend even if you've got a machete to his ding-dong.

We come to Cremita ice-cream shop. The walls are filled with Ricky and Lucy photographs. All ice-cream cones are topped with chocolate bongos.

Francisco orders a triple-decker *guanábana,* mango, and chocolate ice cream. *"¡Delicioso!"* He radiates happiness, and all I want is to blurt out what I must tell him.

I order two scoops of *tres leches* ice cream topped with flan cream.

We stroll the boardwalk savoring our ice creams and reach Papaya's at the end of the pier. The waves are crashing loudly underneath, but I feel them crashing inside me. I'm desperate to speak.

"Listen. Let's forget about dancing. I need to talk *now*," I insist.

"Later. I'm serious. I told you I've got a surprise for you. Don't ruin it."

We finish our ice creams and enter a cloud of

smoke and loud disco music.

There's a bunch of people dancing. Tazer and Felicia yank me by one arm and Jaylene and Rosa by the other.

"Holy pube! What are you guys doing here?"

"Soli asked us to come!" They pull me smack into the middle of the dance floor and whisper to me, "We think Soli's got something planned."

Francisco follows. "I invited Soli and Paublo to come, and a bunch of our friends from work. It's great she invited you guys. The more the merrier." He looks around the club. "Is Soli here?"

Soli, Paublo, and Gisela appear from a cloud of smoke and start dancing with us. We all hug. "I asked Gisela to join us," Soli informs me with a twisted look on her face. She whispers in my ear, "This is your last chance. You know I'm on vacation. Paublo and I are leaving in a few minutes for Key West for two weeks. I won't see you till your birthday. Hope I come back to good news." She kisses my cheek and walks away.

"*Hola*, Laura." Gisela's dancing in front of me, smoothly swaying her curvy hips. Like a magnet, I move slowly around her. We watch each other dance. Francisco walks away to a table to talk with friends he's invited.

Gisela comes closer and smiles right in front of my face. "*Bella,* funny that fate should bring us together again, eh?" I get a glimpse of Francisco, yacking away.

Once the song is over, I force myself to stop dancing.

"Hey, I really love dancing with you, but I've gotta do something important. We'll dance some more later." I kiss her cheek, wave good-bye, and walk away.

Gisela follows me to the table. She hasn't a clue that Francisco and I had been dating. Francisco, being the gentleman that he is, pulls out a chair and invites Gisela to sit with his friends and us.

He introduces everyone to Gisela—I already know them: "This is Sarita, Morena, Taíno, and Gitano."

We all kiss one another's cheeks. I sit next to Francisco, wringing my hands over and over again. I excuse myself and take him to the side.

"Listen, what I need to tell you is that I'm not who you think I am—"

He interrupts. "Laura. You're always on this same note, then you change your tune. Once you see what I've planned for midnight, you'll never say those famous words 'I just want to be friends' again."

It's as if I were talking to a bottle of mustard.

"We need to talk, *now*."

"You must be PMSing." He takes me by surprise and kisses my lips. "If you keep this up, you're going to ruin the surprise. Just have a good time and chill till midnight. Let's go."

He walks away from me. I don't want to make a scene, and so I follow.

We get back to the table. He puts his arm behind my chair and starts yacking away with his buds about some car races he wants to see. I don't want him to put his arm around me; but if he does, I don't want to make a scene in front of his friends. I don't want Gisela to know I had been dating a guy. I have such a strange mix of feelings.

I think I'm finally going nuts.

I talk with his friends awhile. "Gisela is Jaylene's and Rosa's friend." I point to them. "We met at Cha-Cha's, then at Viva's party." I talk about Astro Viva and her antics, and they laugh hysterically.

The conversation twists and twirls. "Let's get away from the blasting music, have drinks outside by the bar, and play pool." Francisco looks at me. "Laura hates alcohol, but it's a special occasion. Come on!"

Everyone stands up except Gisela and me.

"If you drink, I'm not going home with you. Remember that you're driving."

"I'm just going to have *one* drink, Laura." He turns to Gisela. "Let's go!"

"Sorry. I don't drink, either," she says. "I'll take you up on playing pool later."

"Both your losses." He leans in to me and almost kisses my lips. I abruptly turn my face, and his lips smack me a big wet one on my cheek. "Go dance, have fun." He faces Gisela. "Take care of my one and only," he adds. "We'll be back soon."

I turn to Gisela after he leaves and change the subject drastically. "Did you have a good time at Viva's party?"

"It could've been more fun if we had spent some time together."

Damn. This girl is totally into confrontation. I look away from her, toward the dance floor, and catch Jaylene, Felicia, Tazer, and Rosa talking up a storm. They look my way and smile.

My hands are sweaty. I rub them back and forth on my thighs over my tight brown corduroy pants.

Gisela slips off her boots and places her feet on the chair. She hugs her knees and stares at me freely. I watch her out of the corner of my eye. Her index finger and thumb are rubbing the turquoise hanging from a thin green strap around her neck. I find her eyes and shapely body so beautiful, I could die.

"Why did Francisco call you his 'one and only'?"

"He still thinks we're dating." I come clean and tell her a little about my relationship with him.

She sits up straight, holding her knees, looking deeply into my eyes for answers. "Soli didn't tell me you were dating a guy." She puts one foot down and leaves a knee up. "I can't believe you're bi. I thought you were a lesbian through and through." She shakes her head. "I have nothing against bis, but I'm not into dating them again. My ex was bi, and she left me for a guy. From now on I want to be with someone who stomps her foot down and says, 'I'm a *tortillera*!'"

I grab a glass of ice water, gulp it down fast, and munch on some ice. I clasp my hands together around the glass and squeeze it hard. "I'm not bi."

"Are you confused?" she asks earnestly, staring into my eyes, trying hard to figure me out.

"Nope," I answer fast and honestly. I explain why Francisco and I were together for so long. And I add, "I did everything possible to fall in love with him, but emotional closeness just never happened."

She stuffs a balled-up napkin into my empty glass and lowers her other foot to the floor. "But maybe you could have fallen in love with him if you'd gone all the way, like he thought."

I look her smack in the eyes. "Never." My heartbeat is so strong I can hear it. "I *know* it would be that way with every guy, not just Francisco."

"So, why does he still think you're together if you're no longer an item?"

I place the glass on the table and fidget with a napkin. "In the past I ended up letting him talk me into staying with him after I broke it off a few times. After a while he stopped taking me seriously."

She grabs the napkin I'm fidgeting with, rolls it into a ball, and holds it in her hand. "The day I saw you at Cha-Cha's my heart just knew. You had sparks in your eyes, too, but at Viva's party you pushed me away. I've been thinking about you since we first met." Her eyes glow. "Soli shouldn't have invited me over to see you if you're here with the guy you're no longer dating who thinks he's still involved with you."

"Soli doesn't mean to hurt us. I'm psyched she invited you, because I haven't been able to get you out of my mind, either. I was planning on going to see you Sunday morning at Cha-Cha's. I called and found out the schedule of 'my favorite waitress.'" I look deep into her eyes and smile. "I know *exactly* what I want, but first I have to tell Francisco the truth. I need this time with him. Can I call you tomorrow so we can get together?"

She gets up abruptly. "Hey, if I've waited four hundred years and two days for you, I don't see how another day will make a difference, unless I die tonight; then it's your loss." I laugh. She has a wacko sense of humor that's similar to mine. "Okay. I'll expect your call tomorrow. I'm really psyched about seeing you again." She takes out a pen from her back pocket and writes her digits on the palm of my hand. "Good luck." She kisses my cheek and bails.

I head over to Francisco with a jumpy stomach. He's sitting at the bar, talking to his friends, waiting for his turn at the pool table. I edge over to him. He looks toward me with a loving expression.

I sit next to him and whisper in his ear, "I

wasn't in love with Mario. Her name is Marlena."

There's an empty silence between us. Suddenly his expression changes. He looks as if a train is about to hit him. "Are you serious?"

The DJ puts on loud, shrieky music. Francisco's friends are laughing uncontrollably. The smoke and noise bother me. "We'll be right back," I tell his friends, and we walk outside.

He leans his back against a wall. His eyes dart around. The night is dark and windy. He raises his voice. "I can't believe you never told me."

I tell him the entire story, from when I got thrown out of school, till my wanting to fall in love with him so my mother would accept me. "I'm so sorry if I hurt your feelings. I should have told you from day one. I love you as a person, and I love the great times we had together; but I can't fall in love with a guy. It's not you. You're *amazing*! It's *me*."

"You're fucked! Were you faking having a good time with me in bed, too?" I hate that sex is his only focus.

314

"No. I swear! Fooling around with you was fantastic. I loved every minute." I explain about my inability to love guys profoundly and deeply. I let him know it can only happen with girls.

"You used me so your mother would think you're straight and take you back?"

"I'm sorry. I thought for sure, in time, I'd fall in love with you." I give him a friendly peck on the cheek. "Please forgive me. Believe me, Francisco, I wanted us to be in love. I didn't want to hurt you on purpose."

He wipes the kiss with his hand. "Judas!"

"Francisco, please. Don't treat me so mean. You knew all along I was having trouble falling in love. You *never* listened!"

"I have news for you, too," he blurts in a heated tone. "When you said you weren't coming with me to the Bahamas, I invited this chick Lorili, who's hot for me. We hooked up at a hotel and had the time of our lives on a boat. That's why I didn't call you." He would never have come clean if he hadn't wanted to hurt me back. "But it was just raw sex, and you're a better lover, even being a virgin and all. I ended up missing you, and I knew I'd never do that again."

"I guess we're even."

"We're not *even*. Asshole! The reason I wanted to come here is *this*!" He takes out a silver diamond engagement ring from his pocket and shoves it in my face. "But instead you took me for a fool!"

"You knew we were broken up! But if you were in love with me as you say and you slept around, it's weird that you think *I'm* the only jerk here."

"You and I had great times, but you wouldn't go all the way. I'm a man, you know? If a hot girl throws herself at a guy, he's going to go for it. I don't care what any guy says. It's our nature."

"I hope you used protection."

"Shut up! Why did you lead me on?"

I open my mouth to explain, but he growls, "You suck, bitch!" He takes off in the direction of his Jeep.

Diggin' into Love

I called Francisco, but he wouldn't answer. When I went to see him after work, he wouldn't allow me in his house. Ending things in a friendly way, without him hating me, is what I wanted. I feel sad but relieved for both of us. Now he can go on with his life and find a straight girl who really loves him. I finally did what we both needed, but I just wish I hadn't hurt him so much.

I called Gisela this morning and asked her to meet me at the beach before sunset.

Soli drops me off. I get to the edge of the pier and find Gisela. We kiss each other's cheeks and sit, feeling the cool night air blowing on our faces. Our feet dangle down toward the crashing waves. I zip up my wool jacket and rub my hands together.

Gisela smiles. "I can't believe we're finally alone."

"Yeah. I know I haven't acted as if I was totally into you; but I swear, there's something about you that hits me hard."

She takes my hand in hers and whispers, "Now you're talking." Her breath tickles my ear, and I feel a tingling sensation sliding down my spine.

The pier starts to get crowded with people. My heart beats faster as she leans in to me to kiss me. I lean farther away and let go of her hand. "I want to kiss you, but there's too many people around."

"So what. If they don't like it, it's *their* problem. If people don't see more girls together, out and about, doing normal everyday things, they'll never get used to us."

"You're right. I'm just a really private person." I grab her hand and feel butterflies in my chest. "Let's walk on the sand to the water," I say, feeling all mushy inside. We take off our shoes and do just that.

A yellowish light shines over the waves as I sit on the sand, facing the water. She sits next to me, looking out into the horizon. Finally everything inside me feels right. I feel at peace, one with myself and with everything around me. I haven't felt that in a long, long time.

We ask each other a million questions. Unlike most Cuban girls in Miami, she loves horses, hiking, swimming, and camping. And she's really into Cuba, zoology, and anthropology. She confides, "You know, the first day I met you, I wanted to impress you and I chose my words carefully."

"You could have babbled and you would've impressed me." We laugh.

I draw her profile in the sand as we talk about our lives. She tells me, "After my parents got divorced and moved to different states, they allowed me to stay in Miami and live with Abuelita Carmina and Abuelito Jesus."

"Can I meet your *abuelitos*?"

"Definitely. They'll love you."

I ask her about her relationships.

"I was involved with Sonia, the bi I told you about, for a year and a half till she moved to New York. I couldn't leave my grandparents right away. She got upset and instantly found a boyfriend. It's taken me a while to get over her. I wanted to wait till the right person came along."

Just my type of girl.

She asks me questions about my life. I tell her the important things that have happened to me from the day of the Incident until this very moment.

"I've only been in love once, with Marlena, and we were both closeted. I don't know anything about being an 'out' lesbian or going out with gay girls or anything like that." In the sand I sketch her bushy, wild locks flying about her head.

The sun starts to dip slowly into the horizon. Streaks of reds and pinks splash the sky.

I kiss her lips as the orange sun plunges into the sea.

Cozying up next to her, with our arms wrapped around each other, I feel all my pain and confusion melt away. I want to wake up every morning in her arms, with her spicy smell around me.

She kisses me tenderly as I caress her face with my hands. Her kisses float me toward the water, where we are two waves crashing as one. Now that I've found her and she feels the same about me, I never want to let her go.

She kisses my closed eyes. "That was the greatest, most delicious kiss of my life."

I smile. "You're the best kisser in the history of the world."

"Do you believe in Karma?" she asks.

"Not really. It makes no sense that some kids are suffering and dying and serial killers are on the loose, living a grand old life. No way can I believe in Karma; it's criminal to take vengeance on victims now for crimes they don't even know they committed in their past lives."

"Do you believe that everything happens for a reason?"

"Only for *ob*vious reasons. If you stick your foot in fire, it'll burn. I believe we met because Soli, you, and me made it happen."

"You're a cynic and a free thinker. I love that." She gives me a moist kiss on the lips. "I believe we were meant to be. Life is unpredictable, but it seems to be on our side."

I've never heard more beautiful words. I gaze into her eyes. Everything about her moves me deeply. It's so true. Who'd have known that life would bring us together?

Something comes over me. I feel as if I've finally taken off a tight iron mask that I've been wearing all my life. The feeling of freedom is overwhelming; it makes tears pour from my eyes.

She kisses the tears dripping down my cheeks. "You okay?"

"Yeah." I wipe my eyes with my hands. "Just tears of bottled-up happiness."

I feel as if all the puzzle pieces of me have been put back together and I am whole, complete once again. It's not about her; it's about finally letting go of the fear that didn't allow me to be who I truly am. I'm a good person, worthy of acceptance and love.

The day has turned into night. She holds me close, and I breathe in her rain forest smell. Our faces are so close that our noses touch. "I want to stay here forever," I say. "This is our spot. It's got the memory of our first kiss."

We kiss and talk till three in the morning. "Viva must be worried. I've got to go," I explain, and she understands.

We walk hand in hand on the cool sand, leaving behind our footprints to be washed away by the frothy waves.

We get to the parking lot and arrive at her hybrid car. She pushes my hair back behind my ears and fills my entire face with sweet kisses. "Let's get together again tomorrow."

Before I climb into her car, I say, "Tomorrow is ours."

She smiles. "Who knows. Maybe the rest of our lives is ours."

Gay Marriage?

It's December 7, my birthday! I've been seeing Gisela for two weeks. When Soli called from Key West to find out juice, I told her about my breakup with Francisco. I didn't mention Gisela. I want to surprise her.

Gisela turned up at my place with a gift: an Italian film collection. She came with me to buy myself a birthday present with the money I've been saving from landscaping: a mustard-colored 1982 MGB convertible. I bought it cheap from a very old, rich environmental engineer who converted it into a car that runs on one hundred percent electric.

Mami called to wish me a happy birthday. The day after I broke it off with Francisco I told her. She was upset and screamed a bit but calmed down and quickly said, "That eliminates your chances of moving in here anytime soon. But maybe . . . ahhh . . . well . . . we'll see. I'll figure something out."

I didn't ask what she meant by that weird remark. We haven't talked about it since, but today she said I needed to be over at her house at five o'clock, before dinner. I told her I also had a surprise for her. She's going to flip her wig.

Mami's front door is open, and I let myself in. I sniff the air, and it smells like Pedri's favorite orange gelatin.

I sit on Mami's kitchen table, crossing and uncrossing my legs, drumming on the marble counter, waiting for Mami to come out of the shower. I wonder what the surprise will be, but I sure can't wait to tell her mine.

She rushes out of the bathroom wearing a silky green dress, diamond earrings, and pointy high-heeled shoes. She's drenched in makeup and her neck is covered with talcum powder.

I kiss her cheek. She hugs me, and for a moment we're both teary eyed. *"Te quiero, hija. Felicidades."* She hands me a thousand dollars in one-hundred-dollar bills.

"Wow! Thanks, Mami!" I stuff them in my jean pocket. I can't *wait* to surprise Viva behind her back. I'll go straight to the landlord and pay our rent, because she never lets me pay a penny. Then I'll fill the fridge with food that she and Soli love!

Mami runs around nervously, making sure everything in her house is in perfect shape. "Silvina's son, Rogelio"—she's out of breath— "the one who looks *exactly* like Jesucristo, is coming over to meet you now that you're available. He's a lot more handsome than Francisco. That's your surprise. I want you to marry him."

"What?" My heart drops flat on the ground. I should have known better.

She sprays me with perfume.

"Yuk!" I grab the bottle and jump down from the table, coughing, running as fast as I can into the living room, away from the scent. Mami knows perfume grosses me out and makes me nauseous, but she doesn't care. I open the sliding glass doors for a breath of fresh air. I look back at her. "Are you insane about me marrying a guy I don't even know?"

"Close those doors!" she yells from the pantry. "The neighbors!" I slide them shut.

"You've totally lost it!" I've got my hands on my hips, watching her search the cupboards for María cookies.

She finds the cookies at the very end of the shelf and lets out a sigh of relief. *"Ay, gracias a Dios."* She's in my face. "You like hippies and seed-eating vegetarians and those strange environmentalists. He's got long, blond hair and blue eyes. Your children will be blond with light eyes. You just turned eighteen. No man is going to want you in a few years." She pushes me aside. "I got lucky with Osvaldo."

I dump the perfume bottle in the trash when she's not looking. She plops on her embroidered couch with the María cookies on her lap and starts sewing cuffs on Osvaldo's pants. The tiny glasses on the tip of her nose make her look freaky.

"You're nuts!" I open the sliding doors wide and stand outside, looking down at the bay. It's pretty peaceful and quiet out, but I feel chaotic inside. My heart always hurts when I'm around Mami. That's not right. A mom is supposed to love her children no matter what.

Mami hardly chews, and she swallows the first cookie practically whole. "You know it's not normal for a girl to not want to get married. What are you going to do, live with those two women all your life now that you broke up with Francisco?" She stuffs another cookie in her mouth and keeps stitching without looking up.

"Yeah. I'll live with Soli and Viva for the rest of my life. At least *they* love me."

She sticks the needle into the cuff, throws the pants on the couch, takes off her glasses, places them on the coffee table, and storms off to the kitchen. I follow her.

"Don't tell me you haven't changed even after

having had a boyfriend!" She wags her head in disgust. "*¡Ay, mi madre!* You're going to kill me!" The fridge door is open. She's picking at leftover *fricasé de pollo* bones, sucking out the marrow, and drinking orange juice straight from the carton.

Just as I'm about to tell her that yes, I *have* changed, but not in the way she wants me to, the doorbell rings and I freeze. She washes her hands in a fury and runs to answer the door. I feel like leaping off of the balcony into the bay.

In comes a husky blond with icy blue eyes, dressed in a dark blue Italian suit and wearing a long ponytail. Mami kisses him a few times. "He's studying to be a brain surgeon, just like his father. Isn't he the most handsome man you've ever seen, Laura? Didn't I tell you he looks *exactly* like *Jesucristo*? Didn't I?"

"*Jesucristo* probably had dark hair, skin, and eyes, Mami."

"*Ay, chica.* You don't know anything."

Rogelio shakes my hand. Mami makes a mad rush to the fridge and comes back with her specialty flan and a drink. She hands him the dessert.

He accepts, eats it standing up, and raves, "*Qué delicioso*, Marisol. You should open your own bakery."

Mami's cheeks flush so rosy, you'd think she just climbed Mount Rushmore. She hands him the pink *limonada* with a thin slice of lemon.

"*Ay*, Marisol, you're such an incredible host."

Mami leaves us alone. "I've got to finish sewing Osvaldo's pants." Her beach ball butt disappears into the den.

We sit across from each other in the living room, talking about the weather.

He finishes his *limonada*, places it on the coffee table, scoots forward on the couch, and whispers, "Listen. I'll get to the point. I'm gay, too. That's why I'm here."

"What?" I wasn't expecting this.

"*Shhh*. Let's go out on the balcony. I don't want your mom to hear what I'm about to say."

We're on the terrace, looking at the smooth, peaceful waves of the bay. He scoots over to me. "No one knows about me; they think I'm straight. If you want, we can act the part. We'll get married. I'll have my private life; you'll have yours."

I scratch my head. "I can't do that."

He changes the subject. "Hell, Laura, you don't look gay at all. You don't look like those plastic lezzie girls trying to look straight. You're beautiful. I imagined a butch dyke with short hair and a mustache." We laugh. He moves even closer. I can smell his sweet lemonade breath. "I would have never guessed." He grins. "We'd make a gorgeous couple." We laugh uncontrollably.

"I was expecting a straight macho guy who'd be making passes at me. Snap, girl. How come no one's ever found out about you? My mom thinks you're God's gift to girls." He's definitely a hunk.

He squeezes his right arm muscle with his left hand. "No one knows I'm gay because I've had a girlfriend for four years and my boyfriend is a closeted married doctor."

I bite my thumbnail and spit it out. "Does your 'girlfriend' know?"

"It's a cover-up. She's gay, too. The problem is that her new partner is supremely jealous and demanding of her time. Suddenly she can't go out with me anymore."

Our arms are leaning on the veranda railing. He comes so close that our clasped hands touch. I bite my lower lip. "How did you know I was gay?"

"*Ay, mijita,* rumors spread quickly. Every Cuban in Miami knows." He lets loose and gets all queeny just to make me laugh. In a high, lisping voice and with a bent wrist he whispers, "*Ay, chica,* I'll tell my parenths I've fallen deeply, pathionately in love with you, a gay girl, and I turned you thraight. All those thtupid friends of our parenths will love that I've turned you into a dignified hetero. We can walk the threets holding hands, and people will treat you with rethpect."

I belt out a wild laugh. If Mami saw him, she'd fly off the veranda to her death.

He clears his lisp and puts on a serious tone.

"Actually, the truth is that if we don't get married, Laura, we're doomed to live miserable, empty lives. People will always point fingers at us. They'll never stop saying horrible things behind our backs. We'll never be respected like the straights."

I search the sky without answering him. I remember Francisco and what I did to him. If I could take it all back, I would.

I grab my hair with both hands and face him. "That's exactly why we need to come out. The more people get to know us, the more they'll respect us. We're everywhere. If an ER doctor is an out lesbo, will a dying homophobic person stop her from giving him the immediate care he needs? I don't think so. If the lesbo doc saves his life, he'll have more respect for gays. Anyhow, I tried being straight, and I hurt someone really badly. I'll never do that again. We can't let people keep hating us. We need to be in their lives and prove to them that they're wrong."

"I wish I could be as strong as you." He blinks a few times with such tenderness that I feel like hugging him. I come closer and kiss his cheek. He puts his arms around me and hugs me tightly.

We sit on two rocking chairs and talk for a while about his obsession with going to the gym.

"It releases all my tension, and I can sleep like a baby. *Pero, mijita,* let me tell you"—he waves his hand in the air and snaps his fingers twice—"that's where I found Javier, my man." I crack up so loudly, Mami rushes out to us. Rogelio immediately controls himself.

"Act natural," I whisper.

Mami makes the sign of the cross on her chest. "*Ay, Dios mío.* You see? What did I tell you, Rogelio? I knew you were meant for each other."

"*Ay,* Mami, cut it out." She's embarrassing me.

Rogelio starts talking so manly, he sounds as though he took a testosterone shot and was just about to sprout hairs on his chest and back. His back is straight. His hands are crossed over his chest, and he speaks in a husky voice.

"You were right, Marisol; Laura is an absolute dream. She's so ravishing, she should be a model."

"*Ay, mijo,* I've told her that a *milli*on times, but you think she listens? She has to do what *she* wants."

We hang around yacking about all of Mami's

and Rogelio's parents' friends for a while.

Rogelio checks his watch. "Goodness. I have a dinner engagement. I've got twenty minutes to get there." I can tell he made a fake excuse. He can see that I'll never change my mind about marrying him.

We both kiss him good-bye, and Mami invites him back soon. She walks into the elevator with him. I hear the elevator going down, then coming up again.

Mami comes in, smiling widely. "That's the man I want you to marry. He's a good, moral boy, and he comes from a decent family."

I look at her with a serious face. My heart is banging in my chest something wild. I take a deep breath and let it out. "Please listen and try to understand. I'm never going to get married to a man, Mami." I tell her how much I hurt Francisco. "I'm dating a girl named Gisela."

"*¡Ave María Purísima!*" She walks into her bedroom crying and kneels next to her altar of virgin saints. "Please, Virgencita María, what have I done to deserve a daughter like this?"

I stand next to her, no longer feeling ashamed. For the first time I stand up for myself to Mami. I point a finger at her. "No, what have *I* done to deserve *you*?"

"I'm the *best* mother in the world." She bawls and wipes her tears with her hands. "I had you go to a private Catholic school even though it meant working till four in the morning. I took on three jobs just to put food on the table after your father died. I've never thought one minute about myself, only about you and your brother. You're the worst daughter in the world. An ingrate!" She blows her nose in a tissue.

"The worst?" I pace the floor of her bedroom. The memory of her throwing me out of the house flies back to me. "After you found out about me loving another girl, you never, ever cared about me, Mami. Never. You kicked me out of the house just because I was in love with her."

"Don't talk to me about that!"

I shut my eyes really tightly so my tears don't come out. "I tried to fall in love with Francisco just so you'd love me. That's not right." I repeat,

"I'm serious about never marrying a guy, Mami."

"*¡Ay, Dios mío!*" She turns to her small statue of La Virgencita María and with clasped hands she prays, "*Virgencita, por favor, por favor*, why me? How could I have given birth to a degenerate daughter?"

"A degenerate?" My voice quivers. "Mami, Mami. Please understand. I'm no degenerate. I'm your daughter. Why are you being so cruel? All you do is hurt me and hurt me. You have to stop."

She turns to me with such rage in her face, I'm afraid she's going to slap me. "You're sick! Sick and demented. You need a psychiatrist!"

"*You're* the one who needs therapy! I'm going to start supplicating to Santa Barbara so she'll turn *you* gay! How do you like *that*?"

"*Shhh*. The neighbors." She rushes to close the sliding doors.

I calm down. "I've always wanted a mother to understand and support me. But you just can't do it, can you?"

She kisses the teeny San Lázaro medal hanging

from a thin gold chain around her neck. "No. I won't support immorality."

"I can't believe your friggin' saints hate gays."

"Don't disrespect *mis santos* in this house! You hear me?"

"You and your stupid saints! Viva's saints are nicer; they're about love, not hate. No amount of saint worshipping is going to make me marry a guy or turn me straight."

Mami starts sobbing. "You are sick and so are all your friends. That Soli is probably gay, too."

"I'm not *sick* and Soli's *not* gay! I've told you a million times. You've never given Viva or Soli a chance. They love me. You don't love me. Admit it. If I were straight, you'd love me." I'm talking right in her face, but she's looking away. "Viva said I was born 'different,' but she loves me no matter what."

"Don't talk to me about deranged people. Viva's insane! You're going to take me to my grave."

"Mami, I don't want you to suffer. And I don't want to feel any more pain. Let's stop this. Why can't you just accept me and love me for who I am? I'm a good person with good feelings. Why don't you love me, Mami, why?"

She softens up. "I love you too much, Laura; that's why I need you to change. You were never lesbian before that degenerate girl came into your life. Please change so you can come back and we can have a normal family life like we used to."

"I've already tried to change, Mami. It's your turn now. Please, at least *try* to accept me."

"I can't. I don't understand how someone like you came out of me. I'm embarrassed about you, Laura. I can't have you being a *tortillera* in this house. I just can't." Mami walks to the door and swings it open. "When you change, you can come back."

Standing at the door, I gather all the courage I possibly can, and say, "I love you, Mami. I always have. If you can't accept me, that's your problem; but you can't stop me from seeing Pedri again. If you don't allow me in here to see him or take him out, I'll tell Osvaldo the real reason you threw me out of the house."

"¡*Ay, Dios mío!* You're going to kill me! Osvaldo better never, ever, ever find out!"

I take a deep breath and calm myself. "I won't live a lie anymore, Mami."

Sex Goddess and Lesbo Nun

I rush home from Mami's and fling open the back sliding doors. The smells of roasted pork and *cebollitas* saturate the yard. Gabriel is hanging out with his usual bunch of cute Cuban *viejito* friends, barbecuing, playing dominoes, and listening to *son* music. Viva and her cool, open-minded metaphysical girl friends are playing canasta, an old Cuban card game.

"*¡Hola!*" I boom.

Everyone bursts out singing, "Happy bird-day to you. . . ."

Viva rushes to me with open arms and gives me a bunch of *besitos* on my cheeks. "Happy bird-day, Laurita!"

Chispita and Sai Moomi—the fatty bulldog mutt I gave Viva for her b-day—leap up and down, barking like little fiends.

Tazer, Felica, Jaylene, and Rosa greet me with hugs and good wishes. "Gisela's on her way," Jaylene lets me know. "They kept her at work longer than expected."

We're all yacking about that and this when Soli and Diego walk outside. "Sorry we didn't make it on time. Traffic was terrible." She rushes to me. "Happy b-day, Looly!" We hug really tight. I'm surprised she's not with Paublo.

"Wazzz shakin', little bird." Diego gives me a soft kiss on my forehead.

I kiss his cheek. "Great to see you!"

Viva lifts up a lopsided cake, covered with white frosting, chunks of pineapples, shaved coconut, and cherries. "The first cake I ever make, and it be organic. For Laurita, *la mariposita*!"

I blow out the eighteen candles and make a silent wish. *I hope one day Mami accepts me and that Gisela and I last till forever.*

Gabriel starts serving slices of cake on paper plates to everyone lined up in front of the picnic table.

While everybody yaps away, I whisper in Viva's ear with a mouth full of the moistest cake I've ever tasted, "Hey, don't forget to use condoms." I love to bother her.

She slaps my hand. "*Ay*, Laurita, you is such a pain in the butt. You know I is decent. Me no hooking up with Gabriel until we is married." I crack up at her using our lingo.

I lick my fingers. "*Mmmm.* This is so yummy." I sniff her. "Are you becoming a chef behind my back? You smell like garlic and chocolate."

"No. I is getting a cold, so I eat raw garlic and blow-dry my nose with your hair blower." Her belly bulges out and so does her bootie. She's on a diet and has promised everyone that she'd stop eating chocolate, her passionate addiction. She swears up and down like a seesaw, "Me hasn't eaten no chocolates today."

Chispita paws her and a *turrón de chocolate* wrapper flies out of her dress pocket.

"Oh, and what's *this*, a salami sandwich?" She grabs it from me, throws her head back, and shows all her tiny teeth as she laughs, just like Chispita does.

With a swing of the hand, I call Soli to me. I need to talk to her in private. We run inside.

I wrap my arms around her. "I've missed you *so* much! I couldn't *wait* till you got back home." I've never been so happy to see her.

"Bro, you on drugs or what?"

I'm out of breath. "Wass up with you and Diego? What happened to Paublo? I thought you guys were in Key West together."

She fidgets with her nose ring. "I kept a secret from you cuz I knew it would make you happy when you found out." She delves in. "Man, Looly, I left early from Papaya's that night. I knew Francisco was going to propose, and I wanted so badly for you to say no. I couldn't bear thinking you'd marry him. As Paublo and I were leaving for Key West, we bumped into Diego and I couldn't stop talking to him. Before I knew it, Paublo had bounced. He left me there."

"Jesus!" I laugh. "So what *else* could you do but vacation with Diego, right, Hootchi Momma?"

She lets out an ear-piercing laugh. "That's the *best* luck I've ever had! Diego and me got to talking. He broke it off because I wasn't serious about him. He said I have too many guys after me and I didn't treat him special." She shakes her head. "He sure was right, bro. I kind of took him for granted. I don't ever want to lose him again."

I've never heard Soli speak so emotional about a guy. I hug her. "I'm so psyched, Soli. It's about time you find someone you really love; it's such a great feeling."

"Here." She hands me a gorgeous purple photo album decorated with colorful dried flowers. "Mima and I made it before I left for Key West."

"It's so beautiful!" They'd arranged our elementary school pics in order. I leaf through pages of Soli and me making funny faces, me pulling on her pigtails, and me sticking out my tongue behind her back. Memories of sweet times fill my mind.

"Catholic school warped our brains, Looly. Look at us now. I'm a sex goddess, and you're a lesbo nun who was thinking of marrying a guy!"

We laugh our heads off. I can't *wait* to tell her what I've been dying to say.

I squeeze her to me. "This is the *best* birthday present ever!" I take off one of the silver bracelets Papi gave me for my seventh birthday and hand it to her. "Just never lose it, Hootchi Momma."

"What's gotten into you, bro?" She smiles big and places the bracelet on her wrist. "I'll keep it forever. I know it's special." She looks smack into my eyes. "So, did you hook up with Gisela that night? That would be *amazing* news." She snaps off her nose ring and places it in her dress pocket.

"Chill, I'll tell you everything later."

Dark clouds roll in. Everyone rushes onto the back porch. Thunder rumbles loudly, and it starts to pour. I go around opening all the windows.

The electricity shuts off momentarily, along with Gabriel's music. All you can hear are hard raindrops, *tipi-tap-tipi-tap*, and Chuchito, our next-door neighbor's parrot, shrieking, "Happy bird-day to you!"

"Tell me *now*!" Soli is so impatient.

With a huge smile plastered on my face, I fumble around the CD rack for a specific CD and stick it into our CD player. I take a brush from the coffee table, hold it over my mouth like a microphone, and sing along with Diana Ross while waving one hand in the air:

"I'm coming out / I want the world to know / Got to let it show / I'm coming out!" Something inside me suddenly snaps, and I can't hold it in any longer. If I don't say it, I'll explode.

I leap up, throw back my head, and trumpet over the song, "I'm gay! I'm gay!" I lift Soli a few inches in the air and swing her around. "You were right, Soli-Woli! I'm a homo, dyko, lesbo! I'm a *tortillera*!"

"*Wahooo*, you big tort! You finally came to your senses, Looly!"

The *thump-thump* of the rhythmic beat and the raucous stream of wild music set Soli dancing, showing off her bouncy butt and fly moves.

Everybody comes around us and claps to the beat.

I pull Soli to me and spin her around and around, then let her go. I swirl and twirl like a vertigo machine. I take hold of her and steer her.

Soli follows the swinging motion of my wavy hips. "Tell me *every*thing that happened while I was gone!" Her teeny, perfectly lined-up dreads are bouncing all over the place. "Did you tell your mom? Who have you told? *Did* you or did you *not* hook up with Gisela?" She can't stop asking me questions. "Is it somebody else? Tell me! Tell me!"

I don't say a thing. I *love* to keep her in suspense.

Everybody starts dancing. My little mini-scloopi and Sai Moomi run around us in circles, barking, *grrraaawwff-oof*!

I remain silent till Gisela knocks. Finally the moment I was waiting for!

"Come in!" I yell. She walks in, and I throw my arms around her and kiss her lips. We smother each other's faces with kisses. "I could hardly wait to see you again!"

"Me too!" she exclaims.

"Far out! It's Gisela!" Soli blasts. "I knew it!"

We all get into the groove of the music. Gisela undulates her hips, turns, and moves around me with arms as graceful as a butterfly's wings.

I grab Tazer's arm and pull him to us. Viva joins Soli, Gisela, Tazer, and me in a dance by the wall on which I painted her and her favorite saint, Santa Barbara. They're in neon pink lounge chairs, floating on aqua blue ocean waves. They're wearing small, square, tangerine-colored sunglasses and eating grapes.

While on tippy toes, Viva wiggles her bootie outta control. "I no tell Soli that it was Giselita you be seeing. I wanted her to be surprised."

"Sneaks!" Soli blasts.

I tell them what went down at my mom's, then pull Tazer closer to me. "I'll hang with you in the streets now. Sorry I was so dense not to have done that before. Will you ever forgive me?"

"No apologies. I totally get it. Tomorrow we're hitting the town!"

An intense emotion takes hold of me as I wrap myself in Viva's and Soli's arms. "I love you guys. You're my family."

Viva's smile glistens in the dim light of the living room. "You is my little daughter, Laurita. Your mami will come around. You'll see."

"Sisters for life!" Soli remarks.

I glance out the window and see the fog begin to lift. I look at all my friends and Gisela's smile and feel a fog lifting from me, too. I take a deep breath and let it go.

A mild breeze with the smell of rain fills the room. I feel warm and deeply accepted. This is where I belong, loved and understood right down to the bone.

Glossary

Note: the glossary contains
Cuban pronunciations.

abuela (ah-BWEH-la): grandmother

abuelita (ah-bweh-LEE-tah): grandmother

abuelito (ah-bweh-LEE-toh): grandfather

¡Ave María! (AH-veh mah-REE-ah): Cuban exclamation similar to "Holy Mary!"

¡Ave María Purísima! (AH-veh mah-REE-ah poo-REE-see-mah): Cuban exclamation similar to "Holy mother of God!"

¡Ay! (i, *or* AH-e): Oh!

¡Ay, Dios mío! (i *or* AH-e dee-OS ME-o): Oh my God!

Ay, gracias a Dios (i *or* AH-e GRAH-see-ahs ah dee-OS): Oh, thank God

Ay, Jesucristo (i *or* AH-e heh-soo-CREES-toh): Oh, Jesus Christ

¡Ay, madre mía! (i *or* AH-E MAH-dreh MEE-ah): Cuban exclamation similar to "Oh my goodness!"

¡Ay, mi madre! (i *or* AH-E me MAH-dreh): Cuban exclamation similar to "Oh my goodness!"

¡Ay, Santa María madre de Dios! (i *or* AH-e SAHN-tah mah-REE-ah MAH-dreh deh dee-OS): Oh, holy mother of God!

balsa (BAHL-sah): raft

¡Bárbaro! (BAR-bah-ro): Cuban exclamation similar to "Fantastic!"

barrio (BAR-ree-o): Latino neighborhood

bella (BEH-yah): beautiful

bene (BEH-neh): Italian for "fine"

besitos (beh-SEE-tohs): little kisses

bocaditos (bo-cah-DEE-tohs): finger food, appetizers

bolero (bo-LEH-ro): Spanish dance and musical rhythm

caca (CAH-cah): excrement of a child, poop

cacharro (cah-CHAR-ro): old jalopy

café (cah-FEH): coffee

café con leche (cah-FEH cone LEH-cheh): Cuban breakfast drink of espresso, milk, and sugar

cafecitos (cah-feh-SEE-tos): Cuban espresso shots

caldo (CAHL-do): broth

casquitos de guayaba (cas-KEE-tohs deh gwah-YA-bah): guava in light caramel

cebollitas (seh-boh-YEE-tahs): fried onions

cha-cha-cha: sensual Latin dance with complicated rhythms

chica (CHEE-cah): literally means "little girl." Cuban term for "Girl."

chorizo (cho-REE-soh): sausage. Cuban slang for "penis."

churros (CHOO-rrohs): long, deep-fried doughnuts with sugar coating

claves (CLAH-vehs): Latino musical "sticks" that keep the rhythmic timing in beats for the band

Come stai? (COH-meh STAH-ee): Italian for "How are you?"

comemierda (co-meh-mee-ERR-dah): literally means "shit eater." Cuban slang/obscenity similar to "asshole."

croquetas de pollo (cro-KEH-tahs deh PO-yo): chicken croquettes

croquetica (cro-keh-TEE-ca): little croquette

Cubanitas (coo-bah-NEE-tahs): Cuban girls

culito (coo-LEE-toh): tiny butt

degenerada (deh-heh-neh-RAH-da): degenerate

¡Delicioso! (deh-le-see-OH-so): Delicious!

descargamos (des-car-GAH-mohs): we jam (as in a jam session with a band)

¡Dios mío! (de-OS MEE-o): My God!

¡Eh, familia! (EH fah-MEE-le-ah): "Hey, family!"

El Gringo (el GREEN-goh): nickname "The Gringo." Latino nickname for a non-Latino North American.

el hijo de puta (el EE-ho deh-POO-tah): the son of a bitch

el mes que viene (el MESS keh vee-EH-ne): next month

elefantico (eh-leh-fan-TEE-co): little elephant

empanadas de carne (em-pa-NAH-dahs deh CAR-neh): meat pies

enamorada (eh-nah-mo-RAH-dah): in love

espíritus y santos (es-PEE-ree-tos ee SANH-tohs): spirits and saints

¿Estás loca? (es-tahs LO-cah): Are you crazy?

fabuloso (fah-boo-LOH-so): fabulous

factoría (fac-to-REE-ah): factory

flan (flahn): custardlike dessert

fricasé (free-cah-SEH): fricassee

fricasé de pollo (free-cah-SEH deh PO-yo): chicken fricassee

frijoles (free-HO-les): beans

fuiqui-fuiqui (FWEE-kee FWEE-kee): Cuban slang for the sounds bedsprings make when a couple is having sex

¡Gracias! (GRAH-see-ahs): Thank you!

¡Gracias, Dios! (GRAH-see-ahs dee-OS): Thank you, God!

gringo (GREEN-goh) / *gringa* (GREEN-gah): Latino nicknames for a non-Latino North American (male and female forms)

guanábana (goo-ah-NAH-ba-nah): fruit of the guanabano tree, very sweet and white *guarapo* (gwah-RA-po): cane juice

guayabera (gwah-yah-BEH-rah): typical Cuban man's shirt with pockets and vertical pleats

hasta luego (AHS-tah loo-EH-go): good-bye

hola (OH-lah): hello

hola, mariposita (OH-lah mah-ree-po-SEE-tah): hello, little butterfly

¡huy! (OO-ee): Cuban exclamation of surprise similar to "oh!"

invertida (in-ver-TEE-dah): inverted, twisted. Derogatory Cuban slang for "dyke" (*tortillera*).

-ito (EE-toh) / *-ita* (EE-tah): diminutive suffix (masculine and feminine forms)

¡Jesucristo! (heh-soo-CREES-toh): Jesus Christ!

jugo de melocotón (HOO-go deh meh-lo-co-TOHN): peach juice

jugo de naranja (HOO-go deh nah-RAHN-hah): orange juice

la chiquitica más linda del mundo (lah chee-kee-TEE-cah mahs LEEN-dah dehl MOON-doh): the prettiest little girl in the world

la jungla cubana (lah HOON-glah coo-BAH-nah): the Cuban jungle

la luna (lah LOO-nah): the moon

la mejor madre del mundo (lah meh-JOR MAH-dreh del MOON-doh) the best mother in the world

La Vírgencita María (lah VEER-hen-SEE-tah mah-REE-ah): the Virgin Mary

limonada (lee-mo-NAH-dah): lemonade

machazo (mah-CHAH-soh): macho man

Malta (MAHL-tah): brand of nonalcoholic malt drink

mamey (mah-MAY): reddish orange sweet custard, made from a fruit with thick brown skin shaped like a small football

Mami (MAH-mee): Mom

¡Mami, por favor, por favor! (mah-MEE por fah-VOHR): Mami, please, please!

mandarina (man-dah-REE-nah): mandarin

mano (MAH-no): Cuban slang for "man" (as in "No, man!" and "Hey, man!")

¡Maravilloso! (mah-ra-vee-YO-soh): marvelous!

¡Maricones de mierda! (mah-ree-CO-nes day mee-ERR-dah): Faggots full of shit!

mariposita (mah-ree-po-SEE-tah): little butterfly

mariquitas (mah-ree-KEE-tahs): literally means "plantain chips." Cuban slang for "sissy."

mercado (mer-CAH-do): market

merengue (meh-REN-geh): the joyful, lively music and dance from Cuba, Puerto Rico, and the Dominican Republic

merenguito (meh-ren-GEE-toh): confection of sugar and egg whites

mija (MEE-hah) / *mijo* (MEE-hoh): my daughter / my son

mijita (mee-HEE-tah) / *mijito* (mee-HEE-toh): terms of endearment meaning "my little girl" / "my little boy"

Mima (MEE-mah): term of endearment for "Mom." Cubans use either "Mima" or "Mami."

mis santos (mees-SAHN-tohs): my saints

moi (MWAH): French for "me"

muchachita (moo-chah-CHEE-tah): term of endearment meaning "young girl"

mucho (MOO-choh): a lot, a great deal

música (MOO-see-cah): music

No hablo inglés (no AH-bloh een-GLES): I don't speak English

¿Oigo? (OY-go): Hello?

oye (O-yeh): hey

¡Oye, chica! (Oyeh CHEE-ca): Hey, girl!

papas rellenas (PAH-pahs reh-YEH-nahs): stuffed potatoes

Papi (PAH-pee): dad

pastelito (pas-teh-LEE-to): puffed pastry

pastelitos de guayaba (pas-teh-LEE-tos deh gwah-YAH-bah): guava pastries

pastelitos de queso (pas-teh-LEE-tos deh KEH-so): cheese pastries

pendeja (pen-DEH-ha): *pendejo* literally means "pubic hair." Cuban slang for "chicken" or "wimp."

Pero, mijita (PEH-ro mee-HEE-tah): but, girl

peroxido (peh-ROK-see-doh): hydrogen peroxide

piñata (peen-NYAH-tah): jar or pot decorated with fancy paper, filled with candy, and hung from the ceiling. Children pull its string to break it and get the candies.

pipí (pee-PEE): pee

plástica (PLAHS-tee-cah): plastic

platanitos maduros (PLAH-tah-NEE-tos mah-DOO-ros): fried sweet plantains *por favor* (por fah-VOR): please

promesa (pro-MEH-sah): promise

puerco asado (PWER-co a-SAH-do): roast pork

¡Qué cosa más grande la vida! (keh CO-sah mahs GRAHN-deh lah VEE-dah): Cuban exclamation similar to "Unbelievable!"

¡Qué delicioso! (keh deh-lee-see-OH-so): How delicious!

¡Qué horrible! (keh or-REE-bleh): How horrible!

¡Qué loca! (keh LO-cah): What a nut case!

¿Qué pasa, calabaza? (keh PAH-sah cah-lah-BAH-sah): What's up, pumpkin?

¿Qué pasó? (KEH-pah-SO): What happened?

¡Qué rico! (keh REE-co): How delicious!

quinces (KEEN-sehs): Coming-of-age party given to a Latina girl when she turns fifteen (short for *quinceañera*)

salsa (SAHL-sah): diverse and predominantly

Caribbean dance and Latin music

salsita (sahl-SEE-tah): sauce

Santa Bárbara, por favor, por favor (SAHN-tah BAR-bah-rah por-fah-VOR): Saint Barbara, please, please

santero (sahn-TEH-roh): a person who has been initiated as a *Santería* priest and is entitled to work with spirits and *orishas* (deities). *Santería* is a Cuban religion that combines the worship of Catholic saints and Yoruban gods from Africa

¡Santísimo sacramento! (sahn-TEE-see-mo sah-crah-MEN-to): Sacred sacrament!

santos (SAHN-tos): saints

sí (SEE): yes

sombrero de guano (som-BREH-ro deh GWAH-no): fine textured Cuban hat made from the Cuban palm

son (SOHN): style of Cuban country music with roots in the island of Hispaniola *suave y dulce* (soo-AH-veh ee DOOL-seh): soft and sweet

Te quiero, hija. Felicidades. (te KEE-eh-ro EE-hah feh-lees-see-DAH-dehs): I love you, my daughter. Congratulations.

tía (TEE-ah): aunt

timbales (tim-BAH-lehs): percussion kettledrums or timpani mounted on a stand and played standing up

tío (TEE-oh): uncle

tortillera (tor-tee-YEH-rah): Cuban slang for "disgusting dyke." Some political Latina/o gays use this word in a fun, light, and teasing way, just as a North American gay/queer uses the word "fag"; but it is usually derogatory.

tortillera de mierda (tor-tee-YEH-rah deh mee-EHR-dah): dyke full of shit

tres leches (trehs LEH-chehs): Cuban dessert made with sugar, condensed milk, and evaporated milk

¡Tu madre! (too MAH-dreh): literally means "Your mother!" Cuban slang similar to "Up yours!"

tumbadoras (toom-ba-DOH-rahs): congas

turrón de chocolate (toor-ROHN deh cho-co-LAH-teh): nougat paste made of almonds, pine nuts, chocolate, and honey

uno, dos, tres (OOH-no, dohs, trehs): one, two, three

vampiros (vam-PEE-rohs): vampires

viejitas (vee-eh-HEE-tahs): little old ladies

viejito (vee-eh-HEE-to): little old man

Virgen María (veer-hen mah-REE-ah) / *Virgencita María* / (veer-hen-SEE-tah mah-REE-ah): Virgin Mary

y (ee): and

yuca con mojo (YOO-cah cohn MO-ho): Cuban dish consisting of boiled cassava and a sauce made from garlic, onions, and olive oil

Mayra Lazara Dole is an **author** who has **also** been a drummer, **dancer**, landscape designer, **Cuban chef**, hairdresser, and library assistant. She was **born in Cuba** and now lives in **Miami** with her partner, Damarys.

You can visit her online at **www.mayraldole.com.**